Best Wishes

Brian Shaddon

1

DIANN SHADDOX

A
Faded Cottage
A South Carolina
Love Story

DIANN SHADDOX

DIANN SHADDOX

Note:
This is a work of fiction. All characters, places, businesses, and incidents are from the author's imagination. Any resemblance to actual places, people, or events is purely coincidental. Any trademarks mentioned herein are not authorized by the trademark owners and do not in any way mean the work is sponsored by or associated with the trademark owners. Any trademarks used are specifically in a descriptive capacity.

ISBN: 978-0-9912805-1-3
Fourth Paperback Edition

10 9 8 7 6 5 4

Cover Artist: Carl J. Franklin
A Faded Cottage © 2013, Diann Shaddox
Eagle Quill Publishing
Printed in The United States of America

A Faded Cottage

Acknowledgments

I would like to say thank you to my family and friends.

To my family, William, David and Ellen for their encouragement.

To my friends Candy Adams, and Mary Hill "Hilly" Dewey for their support.

Thank you Paula Coopers Matthews, a composer and pianist, for allowing me to use her music for "A Faded Cottage" book trailer.

Thank you John Vaughn, a composer and pianist, for allowing me use his music for "A faded Cottage" book trailer.

To everyone with Essential Tremors, may the power of many voices bring peace to us all.

DIANN SHADDOX

A Faded Cottage

This book is dedicated with love to Randy, my husband.

DIANN SHADDOX

A Faded Cottage

A Charmed Life

Have you ever seen a sunrise?

Or a butterfly born of magnificent colors that glides through the air and even though its life isn't long in this world, its beauty demands our attention if only for a short period of time. I sit thinking of the small feat, a caterpillar evolving becoming Mother Nature's most amazing art.

Just a short time ago, my life was simple and uncomplicated. I was able to bring to life the beauty of the world; the short flight of the butterfly, the raging waters of an ocean, and the grandeur and simplicity of a sunrise. Since I was a young boy, I was blessed with the ability to turn blank canvases into superb masterpieces.

My life has been one of marvel. I've won numerous awards in the art world, and I've made more money than any man deserves. I have given speeches before huge corporations, Heads of State and started my own corporation. I was born of nobility and I'm what most would call an aristocrat. I've lived in the city of New York, in my penthouse at 985 5th Ave., with its spectacular views of Central Park most of my life. I've become accustomed to servants seeing to my every whim since I was a baby. I've traveled the world meeting Kings and Queens.

But, it seems money can't buy everything.

With all of my money and prestige, I lost the most precious thing to me, my ability to paint great masterpieces. I have done my share of asking why, a question without an answer, of how a man of my caliber could lose control of his hands and body.

I believed I was going insane, maybe I did. My world began to crumble when a simple act of signing autographs with my trembling hands brought snickering and sarcastic comments at my art studio. I heard my servants, who were well compensated for their work in my home; make disparaging remarks in quiet whispers, as they would leave a room. However, the worst of all came when the critics began spreading the word that my once spectacular paintings looked as if a child had painted them. I became overwhelmed, a hopeless bitter man trying to hide away from the stares and whispers. Believing my life was over, I left my home in New York, and I moved to a small town on the coast of South Carolina to disappear from the world.

I moved into a faded cottage on 11 Gull Lane that September 16th, 1982. I'd like to say I discovered my amazing cottage, faded, worn, sitting on the beach; a cottage so similar to me, flawed, but really the cottage found me. It was another ironic twist in my life. The cottage, with its incredible views of the ocean and its mystery, pulled me in from the first time I laid eyes on it. I packed a few things, mostly small paintings I'd painted when I was a young man sitting on this same beach, storing all of my other things that didn't matter to me anymore.

I sit this cool January day, 1983, in the old rocker on the back porch of the faded cottage. This has become my routine each morning, watching the sun as it rises in the sky spreading colors over the deep blue water of the Atlantic Ocean.

A Faded Cottage

I cradle my journal in my arms. I look down seeing the unsteady hands of an artist, trembling, not even able to grip the ink pen. So, why must I write down my story for others to read and who would care?

First and foremost, this isn't a story of my entire life. Rather it's a story of only two weeks, a story of an endless love. How could such a short period of time have possibly altered a man's life? I only have my answer, the answer of a simple man. I have faith that love isn't only counted in years, but days and hours. Hours can change a man's direction even a chance meeting, leading us on a journey.

But my story didn't begin that beautiful fall day when I moved into this cottage, the warm sun radiating down. My story began on a cold blistery day in December. Tears brim in my eyes remembering that Saturday morning, every detail fresh in my mind.

The back of my hand wipes the wetness from my face; not deterring my scribbling words of how love changed my life from an angry and resentful man begins to flow onto the paper.

Laying the pen on the table next to the rocker, I cuddle the journal full of my dreams. Most people think I'm unrealistic, a romantic, but I've seen the strength, the power of love. And I have faith that love can conquer all. If there's one thing I've learned, I will never give up, no matter what fate has in store for me.

I lay my feet flat on the porch floor, the rocker stops moving, and the journal opens to its beginning. I sit quietly for a few minutes. My eyes stare out into the great ocean and I hear the waves gently splashing on the beach smoothing the sand, repeating a never-ending cycle of life. My eyes are pulled downward seeing the scrawled words as I begin to read…

DIANN SHADDOX

A Faded Cottage

Ghosts from the Past

"Happy Birthday, dumb-ass!" Brenton Quaid Witherspoon's words echoed into the roar of the waves. His heart pounded in his chest as the cold mist circled and engulfed him. The wetness he mopped from his face with the sleeve of his jacket revealed the eyes of a world-renowned artist, known for his superb paintings of the sea.

Quaid watched the dark, cumulus clouds as they grew in the threatening sky, showing colors of grey, black, dark blue and a hint of orange bleeding through from the morning sun. His trembling hands reached out in front of him tightening into fists. His throat constricted, anger grew, with the realization he would never bring the beautiful scene to life on canvas ever again, merely in his dreams.

He reached in his pocket. A folded newspaper clipping slid out. *Brenton Quaid Witherspoon is a prolific artist, producing over 3,000 original works in his lifetime.* The paper crinkled in his fist flying out into the waves. "I was," he screamed, "a prolific artist!"

On this chilly Saturday morning, December 18th, 1982 Quaid, a man of medium height with gray sprinkled in his thick, dark hair not showing his age, continued his daily walk along the fresh white sand next to the Atlantic Ocean. He rounded the curve and stopped. He stared down the long seashore. He was alone, just him and the one seagull he'd fed so many times. He'd hoped ole Amos would be down past the curve fishing, his morning routine since Amos had retired, but even he hadn't ventured out on the damp morning.

Quaid's hands tucked in his jean pockets and he twirled around in a half circle. The blustery sea breeze hit him straight in his face kissing his lips as he tasted the salt. Quickly, he ducked his head trying to hide from the gust of the cold wind.

A deep breath of salty air sucked into his lungs. A wave of pain came over him, thinking about last year, when his life had screeched to a sudden stop.

Now, at the age of fifty, this was Quaid's new life, living in an old framed cottage at 11 Gull Lane, a cottage with a sagging porch, tattered shutters, and worn paint sitting on the beach in the small town of Hathaway Cove. Hathaway Cove, a tiny fishing town of only five hundred including dogs, sat secluded, nestled among the small barrier islands along the coast of South Carolina away from civilization. A quaint, southern town known for its tales of shipwrecks had brought many tourists trying to discover pirate's treasure that they believe was still hiding in the deep blue waters surround this picturesque island.

Quaid slowed his pace and his eyes stared up at the old cottage securely tucked in behind the sand dunes. The quaint cottage, it's once beautiful boards now weathered and timeworn, had sat on the South Carolina coast withstanding hurricanes and storms for over eighty years. Two porches dressed in hand-carved wooden trim spread across the back of the small cottage facing the Atlantic. It was a perfect place to sit and watch the sunrise and a wonderful place to enjoy peaceful evenings listening to the waves serenade the beach.

At the young age of five, Quaid's love of painting had been born on the quiet beach of Hathaway Cove. Time moved on and his passion for painting grew, as did his ability to bring brilliant colors of the Atlantic Ocean to life. He could turn a lonely wave into a superb painting showing the strength of the wave, its fury, its beauty, bringing nature alive. His yearning to paint never failed him, but his hands had now deserted him.

Quaid had lived all over the world, but now he wanted to hide away from the world and moving to a small cottage on Gull Lane, leaving his comfortable life, his family, and his friends back in New York, seemed the perfect solution.

The calmness of Hathaway Cove wasn't the only reason Quaid returned. The faded cottage pulled him in the first moment he laid his eyes on it. Not only was the cottage so like him, its spirit broken, but the mystery it held stirred old feelings in Quaid, bringing back memories of one summer thirty years ago, the summer he was a boy of eighteen. The summer he found his one and only love, his best friend. The same summer he let her go. It was a memory that had haunted him for three decades.

His lone steps in the damp sand left a trail guiding him home along with the rotting seaweed snaking along the shore of the churning waters of the stormy Atlantic.

Thoughts of his life flowed in his mind. Quaid married when he was a young man of twenty-one, a marriage of convenience. Or duty. Either way it wasn't for love, but it wasn't for the lack of trying to make it work that the marriage didn't last long. He made his life and his young bride's life miserable. She was such a beautiful young woman in every way a man would desire, but they both understood a ghost lived in his heart and his new wife wasn't willing to share him. They went their separate ways and Quaid found many other women willing to overlook the ghost, understanding he would never love them.

The tall sea oats swished against his pant legs as he stepped upon the wooden boardwalk and the crunching of the sand on the worn path showed the way to the steps of the porch.

His hands slip from his pockets. His fingers wrapped around the smooth railing as he stepped up the scuffed steps as they moaned with the weight of his body. He stopped at the top of the steps taking in all that was around him. An old-fashion, slatted wooden swing hung on the other side of the porch, worn from many years of use. Two tattered, wicker rockers sat at the edge of the porch, swaying back and forth in a steady rhythm, as if someone was gently pushing them. A smile finally came over his face as he stared at the empty rockers. Maybe ghosts from the past were enjoying the quietness of the morning. Oddly enough, that gave him a comforting feeling.

Quaid pulled in a deep breath of salty, sweet air and his fingers combed his thick, wild hair from his face. A gust of wind hit his back. The sea breeze was somehow whispering to him, as if it were talking, telling tales from the past.

His fingers turned the doorknob of the weathered-faded door, the one he'd been meaning to paint. His head shook back and forth as the irony hit, him being an artist.

His fingers flicked the light switch and the old ceiling light turned on in the small kitchen. The smell of fried bacon lingered in the air, a treat for his birthday.

His jacket shook sending sprays of water droplets from the morning mist floating to the floor. He hung the wet jacket on the hook next to the backdoor to dry. His shoes slipped off scooting them to the side. Toes wiggled sticking out the holes of the navy socks reminding him of the satire of his life. Quaid's friends back in New York would think he had gone mad if they could see him now in his weathered clothes, not designer suits.

He shivered, hurrying into the living room to the fireplace with its red brick hearth blackened from many fires. He knelt down in front of the fireplace pulling the mesh screen open showing the perfectly laid logs on the metal grate. The lighter clicked and flames shot out, letting the kindling under the logs catch fire, hissing and popping as dry wood took flame.

16

A Faded Cottage

Quaid pulled himself from the floor, laying the lighter next to the clock on the mantel. His body didn't move, but his eyes peered up. The fire's amber glow in the dark room brought the incredible painting hanging above the brick fireplace to life, a painting he hadn't seen in over thirty years, the mystery the cottage held.

His eyes took in every inch of the painting. The waves were so realistic he could taste the salt on his lips, just as he had earlier. The sand in the painting had footprints and the sea grass fluttered in a soft breeze. The sky was baby blue and the water had an emerald touch, along with the dark, bluish-green hue telling of its depth. Feeling the warmth from the sun's rays, a smile emerged on his face. He stared deep into the painting seeing the anonymity it held, knowing only one other person knew the painting's secret hidden deep inside. The mystery of the painting swirled in his mind and he hoped he'd soon find his answer, of why the painting had been left in this old cottage.

The squashy, overstuffed chair moaned as he sat down. His feet lay on the frayed ottoman and his toes wiggled peeking from the dress socks. The rain continued to fall steadily hitting the metal on the roof of the fireplace, pinging and drenching the cottage. The fire's flames flickered dancing across the walls, giving off peacefulness in the darkened room.

This old cottage wasn't very big, tiny compared to his large four-bedroom condo in New York, with two small bedrooms, one up, one down. It only had one full bath, but it was what he'd been looking for with large windows letting in the bright sunshine into each room. The cottage needed some work. Its wooden floors were scuffed from years of use with paths to and from each room and its flowery faded wallpaper showed where pictures had once hung. Quaid could deal with the faded and timeworn look that gave the cottage its character, making it home.

The only story Quaid knew about the cottage was of its beginning. Mr. and Mrs. Carlton Brookshire of the distinguished Brookshires from New Canaan, Connecticut, built the cottage at the turn of the century. Mrs. Brookshire was a frail young woman in bad health and had been told by her doctor she needed to leave the harsh winters of Connecticut. Mr. Brookshire, who doted on his wife, was happy to oblige. Harold Todd, a man who constructed most of the newer homes in Hathaway Cove, was hired to build the small cottage and by Mrs. Brookshire's instructions, large windows were added across the back of the home so she could sit in her bedroom and stare out at the Atlantic Ocean. The two porches on the back of the home had to be large by comparison to the size of the home, so she could entertain her friends on beautiful sunny South Carolina days.

The Brookshire family moved into the cottage when Carlton, Jr. was a young boy of eight. After the death of Carlton Brookshire Sr., Mrs. Eula Brookshire stayed, never leaving the small cottage for even a day, until she died in the summer of 1955. Carlton Jr. didn't have the heart to sell the cottage after his mother's death. Carlton Jr. kept the cottage as his vacation home, until his death at the age of seventy-five in 1967. It seemed no one in the small town knew the answer to the mystery, of who bought Mrs. Eula's cottage from the Brookshire estate.

A black and white portrait of the newly built cottage had been left in the bedroom hanging next to the window. The cottage sat with its freshly painted white boards and its porches level, not leaning as they were now. The squatted oak to the side of the cottage was young in the photo, just beginning its life.

Quaid moved the portrait of the cottage into the living room so he could sit and stare at it just as Miss Eula had done so many years ago, believing the spirit of Miss Eula was still in this cottage.

Quaid's eyes moved from the portrait to the clock on the mantel and he watched as it ticked meticulously slow. His life of deadlines was gone and now he had an overabundance of time to think, to question his life. This was now his life, living alone in a small faded cottage in a small town hiding away from people. Gone was the bustling city of New York, Broadway plays and eating at the finest restaurants, wearing the best clothes, staff waiting to see to his every need. That was the reason he'd left his massive condo that overlooked Central Park in the first place. Quaid had become a prisoner in his own home. He couldn't leave his condo and face people out in public and he didn't want anyone staring at him, whispering, snickering when he would spill or drop something.

A paintbrush lifted in his hand. The quivering grew in his fingers, which twitched uncontrollably. The wooden stick snapped in half. His convulsing hands reached out in front of him, clutching them together. His knuckles turned white with the force of his anger. The weightiness of his chest squeezed tight, taking air from his lungs as his throat tightened. His life was slowly slipping away. Each minute he was becoming a shell of the man he once was, but it wasn't age draining his life. He was living without passion, the drive for life. His soul was dying along with his quivering body.

He placed his elbows onto the wide arms of the old chair. His hands laced together and his right fingers wiggled against his left hand, missing any form of a ring. Quaid's moist eyes pulled to the empty overstuff chair next to him. His life flowed like an old movie in his mind thinking of his biggest mistake, his one what if. So crisp in full color reliving the year he found his one and only love.

A piece of wood crackled loudly, pulling his eyes back to the fireplace where they stopped only for a second before traveling to the painting hanging above. The unique painting pulled him in deep into its memory, the mystery it held, bringing back his ghost so clearly from his past...

DIANN SHADDOX

A Faded Cottage
A Chance Meeting

It was the beginning of summer in 1952 and the Witherspoon family had arrived in the small town of Hathaway Cove for their yearly summer vacation. This was a great year for Quaid. He'd graduated from a private high school in New York, a cocky young boy wanting to be a man. He had dark skin like his Italian mother, along with the wild, dark head of hair like his father. Quaid's eyes were deep blue with just the right size nose and a strong jaw line. He had so many dreams of becoming a great artist and marrying Karen, a girl from the right family he'd met at the country club. He played basketball throughout the winter, along with his father's favorite sport, tennis, keeping him in top shape. A perfect life, laid out as his father had taught him. Or so Quaid thought.

That warm day in late May, the station wagon parked in the gravel drive in front of the soaring 1800's plantation home a few houses down on Gull Lane from Miss Eula's cottage, was finally unloaded of its luggage.

Louise, Quaid's mother, a tiny woman, was busy running around the three-story home. McKinley Witherspoon, Quaid's father, a tall, handsome man with the same deep blue eyes, was in the living room with Bradley, Quaid's younger brother. Nothing was impulsive for the two of them planning precisely each day of the family's vacation.

The first day of summer vacation was amazing. Quaid stepped out of the old three-story home onto the lower porch. The warmth of the sun radiated down onto the wooden planks and the salt laden breeze stung his face.

Quaid's loafers slipped off and he laid them on the scraped steps of the porch. His feet sank into the heated sand making him shiver in the cool ocean breeze as he walked across the hilly dune.

He strolled casually, letting his body soak in the sun's rays. The sandy beach was quiet. He stayed next to the cool water smelling the scent of salt and seaweed, each tantalizing his senses. Chilly waves were unrelenting with their silky touch smoothing the sand, splashing at his feet, enticing him.

His foot kicked the sand as he walked and he let it fly into the air, a habit he'd started when he was a young boy. He stopped walking and studied the tiny specks gently falling back to the ground but something else caught his eye.

Quaid stared down the long, winding beach. His body froze when he came near; a smile covered his face, along with a sensation of heat and redness, but it wasn't from the sun.

Lying in front of him on a colorful beach towel, in a tiny, deep blue bikini was a young girl. Her straight, light brown hair flowed against the side of her head. She was lying on her stomach with her face turned away from him and he watched as she took in slow, soft breaths.

"You know," Quaid said in a quiet voice, not wanting to startle her. "Your back is getting red."

The young girl's head gradually turned toward him and dark green eyes peered out from under long bangs. "What business is it of yours?"

"None," he replied, continuing to stare. "But you're going to be sorry tonight."

"I'll be fine. Stop staring at my butt!" the young girl demanded shaking her head letting her long hair fly in the gentle breeze.

Quaid flinched, taken aback for a moment by how blunt she was then he started to laugh. "Actually, I guess I was staring. Nice butt." He relaxed. The heat of his face disappeared but his eyes didn't deter.

The young girl sat up, wiping the perspiration off her face with her towel.

Quaid's face warmed once more turning a dark crimson color when he saw how beautiful she was with those round green-jeweled eyes, oval shape face, and perfect little nose.

"You're new around here," she declared, cupping her hand, trying to cover her squinting eyes from the sun. "I guess you're one of the vacationers who stays all summer?" She became quiet, turning her head to hide from the sun.

"That would be me," he replied. "You're not a local, are you?"

"I am now. My mom and I moved here last fall. You know, I have been warned about guys like you. There were a few guys like you last spring. Would you stop staring at me," she snapped, stretching her arms out wide, "at least you could play the part of not noticing."

"Why, you already know I'm staring," he said smugly, "and I have to say I do like what I see."

"Great," she said irritably shaking her head, "an honest lunatic."

"Look," Quaid said moving closer. "You don't have to worry about me. I have a girlfriend back in New York."

"Then why are you staring?"

"It doesn't hurt to look," Quaid declared proudly.

"Oh…Boys. You're all the same." She stood flinging her towel in the air, letting granules of sand fly.

"Your burn is going to hurt tonight and you are going to need a lot of lotion on your back when you get home," Quaid announced. His head nodded yes. "Awe...I see," he said amused. "You fell asleep, didn't you? You were asleep when I walked up. Good thing I was staring."

"I was just resting, with my eyes closed. I'll be fine," she said, pursing her lips together. Her feet slipped into multicolor flip-flops. Slowly, she trudged up the path to the dune with her hair flying behind her. Her head turned around. "Stop staring at my butt!" she yelled back to him.

He shrugged his shoulders. "I can't help it. Hey...what's your name?" he shouted back to her, waving his arm in the air.

"Sandy!" she yelled. A grin came on her face as her towel swung flapping in the wind.

"I'm Quaid," he shouted watching the beautiful girl disappear over the dune.

Thinking most of the night about his meeting the day before, Quaid was up early the next morning making his way back to the beach letting the water splash at his feet. The warm sun was rising over the water, showing incredible colors exploding in the sky. He came around the curve. He stopped walking. His eyes caught a glimpse of someone sitting on the beach.

He stared down into those green eyes, the eyes he had seen time and again in his mind during the night. The young girl's skin was bronze, but her back was lobster red. She didn't say anything, but slowly her hand smoothed the long towel on the soft sand, patting it gently.

Quaid scooted in next to the young girl. He sat quietly not able to find his voice. She smelled so sweet like a flower after a summer rain. He had never been nervous around any girl, but Sandy made his heart pound so loud, he was afraid she would hear.

Her head lean back gazing up at the blue sky and her long hair swayed in the gentle breeze.

A Faded Cottage

His eyes stayed awestruck staring at her. She was like a locked diary hidden with secrets, mesmerizing him. He smiled to himself, hoping he would become the keeper of the key and he would be able to unlock her heart.

He leaned back on his elbows, listening, letting her talk. She didn't hold back, saying what she thought as if they had known each other for years. He relaxed with each word that flowed softly from her lips. He sat watching her every move. How she twisted her hair with her fingers and how she would smile making her dimples show. Then, he began talking about his own dreams, telling secrets he hadn't told anyone.

That one summer day Quaid became a man, not from lust, but from love. One lone day seemed like a year but passed in minutes. They were lost in their own world, walking along the beach and around the small town. Time vanished and the day faded away to evening ending way too soon. His arms wrapped around her as he walked her home. Before they made it to her door, he slowly pulled her next to his body. Those green eyes peered up at him with the same spirit for life he'd seen yesterday. He tenderly brushed her hair from her face and his body stiffened staring into eyes he was certain could see into his soul. His nerves from the morning had disappeared when his lips pressed against hers; holding her snug, touching her soft smooth skin.

One day grew into months, two and a half wonderful months spent together, their bodies and souls blending into one person. Quaid had never felt emotions like those any other time in his life.

Quaid sighed as his shoulders tensed. It was a motion picture he replayed in his mind and it was difficult to relive his dream. But, this wasn't a dream; it was his life, a life never to be. The ghost from his past had haunted him all these years. He had tried time and again to forget that one summer and the love he had lost, but his mind was incapable of letting the young girl go.

Quaid's head slowly tilted back against the soft chair. He understood he'd spent his life searching and trying to replace the passion he'd felt so long ago. He'd been a fool to leave her.

His trembling hands he held in the air and his face became tense. Now, he'd lost both of his loves.

Tears brimmed in his eyes as so many memories flowed through his mind. He wasn't ashamed to cry, it was his punishment of sorts. The anger had long been gone, but the heartache had never disappeared, knowing their one meeting so many years ago had altered his life forever. His quivering hands rubbed tightly together. In the silence of the room, he said her name over and over. "Sandy."

A Faded Cottage

Tears from the Past

Friday evening, December the 17th, was as usual, making it home from work about six o'clock. Sandy flung her heels in the air, slipping on her cuddly house shoes in the shape of a cat, complete with whiskers, a gift from a friend. She reached into the refrigerator and lifted out the frosty pitcher. She poured herself a nice glass of herbal lemonade, a concoction she'd created. She fixed a small snack, given she wasn't very hungry. The medicine she took killed what appetite she had left.

The threadbare recliner tilted back as she gently rubbed Snowball, her white, fluffy cat, who was sitting in her lap.

Her condo wasn't overly decorated. Rather it was just like her life, very simple. Material things didn't matter to her, but living things, plants and animals. That was another issue.

She lifted her book from the round table sitting next to her chair and relaxed until the phone rang. Hearing his name, a name she hadn't heard in thirty years, her book fell to the floor with a thud.

The name repeated itself in her mind. Quaid Witherspoon. Her dear friend KC from high school told her Quaid's story, of how he'd moved back to Hathaway Cove, and was living in the cottage, yes, the cottage on Gull Lane. The one she'd once owned. Quaid was wondering about her and it seemed Quaid was asking questions.

She jumped out of the recliner. Snowball leaped to the floor. Sandy's fingers gripped the phone tightly and her house shoes swished on the carpet as she paced back and forth in her small living room.

She stared out the living room window. Her eyes stayed fixed seeing the world in its bare state with its brown leaves covering the once green grass, dormant just as her life. Emotions were overflowing, a happiness of sorts then sadness, and then anger began to build.

"How dare he want to see me after all these years after leaving me like he did?" Her eyes closed, remembering his gentle touch holding her close as they sat on the sandy beach. " Why," softly fell from her lips, letting her anger slip away.

Life had been full of ups and downs for Sandy Jamison. She finished college as planned and became a Botanist for the state of South Carolina. Her passion for her plants and life hadn't altered, but maybe her passion had been misguided all these years.

Life hadn't been easy for her growing up with only her mother, never knowing her father. Her father left when Sandy was a baby, making Sandy's mother a bitter woman, never trusting any man. Sandy wondered if her mother's feelings had rubbed off on her and maybe she'd pushed Quaid away.

The bedroom closet door swung open. On the top shelf was an old scrapbook filled with memories of their one summer, a summer a lifetime ago. Pictures, tickets to the state fair, the one special dance and the many times sitting on the beach, now lay in front of her.

Sandy sighed. The best picture of all. Their one special place, Turtle Island. It was where they hid away from the world. Her eyes filled with tears dropping onto the pages below, pages she hadn't seen since the summer she turned eighteen. Her hands gripped one of the old papers, slipping it from the plastic sleeve, a drawing of the two of them sitting on the beach.

Quaid's arms held her tight and the moon shone onto the water. The realism of the drawing made her shudder feeling the coolness of the water and the night air. At the bottom of the page was his signature. It was one of many drawings he'd given her. Sandy had kept them all so she would never forget him.

She closed the frayed, plaid book, bringing it to her chest and smiled, his enticing blue eyes fresh in her mind always on her. He was the only man in her life who'd ever made her feel so special, so loved.

She grabbed a small suitcase from the bottom of the closet. She had to know her answer if any of their summer was real. Her one regret in life was staring her in the face. Sandy threw clothes into the suitcase without thinking about the consequences.

The clock on the nightstand glared eleven o'clock. Her head leaned against the bed's headboard reliving that one summer when she was a teenager.

"That blasted summer," she cried out into the quiet bedroom, squeezing her pillow to her chest as tears dripped down her face, each detail of that summer fresh in her mind.

Sandy knew life wasn't fair, but something was compelling her to learn the truth. If she could reclaim a part of her past, maybe she could find peace.

Sandy woke early the next morning. The pillow snugged tight in her arms, stained where black tears had fallen. Mornings made life easier with the darkness fading and the light from the sun creeping into the room.

December 18th, the date was etched in her mind. It was exactly one week before Christmas, Quaid's birthday, coincidence, or fate.

She grabbed her jeans and a new sweater with multicolor swirls, hurrying to the bathroom. She leaned against the side of the tub watching the warm water flow from the faucet, swirling, just the same as her thoughts swirling in her head. Her hair swished around in the water. Her razor lifted from the shelf, one she hadn't used in weeks, since it was winter, no need to shave, but this was different, like a date.

Her body slid into the warm water. Her mother's voice played in the quiet room. "Now, Sandra, don't start making this more than it is. He's not like you. He's from another social class and those wealthy people don't care for people like us." The water covered her head as she slid deep into the tub drowning her thoughts, her mother's words. Her mother was still telling her what to do.

She stepped out of the tub and pulled her hair from her face. She stared into the mirror, studying her body. Her breasts sagged, not as perky as they once were, but still nice and round. Her hand rubbed her stomach feeling only a slight roundness. A smile appeared. She could see the curviness of her hips. Many men had mistaken her for a much younger woman.

Her thick brown hair began to dry. Her finger quickly began putting makeup on. Makeup she didn't use often, no reason to. Her special pair of jeans slipped on, the ones that fit just right. Her eyes peered into the mirror hanging on the back of the closet door. She grinned. She still looked like the young girl from so long ago, save for a few more wrinkles and a few more pounds, but the curves where still in the right places. Not bad for a woman soon to be fifty.

The lid snapped on her suitcase. Sandy had to keep moving or she wouldn't have the courage to leave. Scooping Snowball up in her arms, she gave him a hug, whispering that she loved him and Mrs. Stone would be seeing to him. The cat leapt from her arms and she grabbed an apple and a can of soda along with her purse and hurried to the door. Her hand hooked the handle of her suitcase and closed the door behind her as she stepped out to her car, moving forward.

A Faded Cottage

What-ifs

Quaid's body shivered with the memories still flowing in his mind remembering his ghost from the past. An hour soon passed. He stood from his chair going into the kitchen. The knob on the stove turned with a click letting blue flames shoot up. Quaid placed a teakettle full of water on top of the burner. He pulled a wooden box full of herbal teas, a gift for his birthday, from the cabinet before reaching for his favorite mug.

The blue curtains on the kitchen door slid to the side. This morning the sea was churning with a vengeance and its power had combined with the storm's fury. The white caps pointed like fingers ready to grip any ship in their wake. Quaid loved to watch the water come alive, pulsating with excitement, a painting waiting to be born.

The teakettle's whistle sang in the quiet. The tall flames turned off. He sat his mug in the sink, a trick he'd learned. He poured the boiling water into the beige mug, not worried about splashing the hot liquid. He dropped the teabag into the water, letting the tea steep. He cupped the mug in both of his hands. The warmth didn't bother him, but cold was another issue. He cautiously carried the hot liquid into the living room trying to keep his hands steady, a tough job now.

A book lay on the table next to the chair. Quaid was a sucker for stories of happy ever after. He'd told himself he'd be able to catch up on his reading, but his first and only book thus far sat, not even the first chapter read. The words would flow from the pages and he would see images coming to life. The book would then be placed back onto the table. The images in his mind were from his past, not from a book.

Tires crunching the gravel in the driveway out front quickly brought Quaid's thoughts back to the present. He pulled himself up from the chair and headed for the front door.

"Happy birthday, Quaid," a tall, thin man announced, stepping up to the porch with a sack of groceries and a gift in his arms.

"Levi, get in here before you get soaking wet," Quaid called out. He backed up, letting the man into the room taking the sack full of groceries setting them on the kitchen table.

"Boy, the rain is coming down out there in buckets. I thought the storm was going to move on, but it's gotten worse," Levi offered. "Here," he handed Quaid the wrapped gift dotted with raindrops, Happy Birthday all over the paper in bright, colors, and a big blue bow sitting on top.

Quaid stared. "How did you know it was my birthday? I never said anything."

Levi laughed. "Oh, but you did over thirty years ago when you were here for Christmas vacation with your family, the year you turned sixteen." Levi turned from Quaid, carefully hanging his wet jacket on the hook behind the front door.

"You remembered from way back then?"

"No, not me, Jenny. She doesn't forget anyone's birthday. You wouldn't let her have a party then or make a big deal out of your birthday," Levi said, a big grin spread across his face. "So now, at least you get a present."

"She sure is amazing," Quaid said, hugging the present in his hands, "and you're a lucky man."

"I sure am."

"How about a cup of tea?"

"Naw," Levi shook his head, "but I would take a soda."

"I also..." Quaid stopped walking. He turned back towards Levi with a big smile on his face. "Have some homemade cookies, peanut butter, and chocolate chip."

"Well now, sounds good to me, but don't tell Jenny. She keeps my sweets to a minimum.

"Thanks for picking up the groceries," Quaid called out from the kitchen.

"Sure, no problem, but Quaid someday you'll have to get back out in public."

"Someday," Quaid moaned.

The plate of cookies sat on the table between the chairs.

"Alright," Levi moaned with his mouth full, "they're delicious, where did you get'em?" Levi stopped chewing, giving Quaid a look. "You didn't bake them yourself?"

"No, I haven't become Suzie homemaker, not yet. Karrie brought them over the other day."

"Karrie, oh," Levi mumbled, a grin came over his face. "Did she know it was your birthday?"

"No, she just stopped by. Feeling sorry for me, I guess. Amos didn't get out in this mess today. I thought he might be out fishing early this morning before the storm moved in."

Levi settled into the other overstuffed chair next to Quaid. "Naw, Mama won't let him out of the house if it's too damp and cold. She doesn't mind if it's warm and rainy."

"It's a mess out there. I went for a walk early this morning, but I didn't stay out long, the wind was too blustery and it began to drizzle."

"So, Karrie is stopping by," Levi remarked, grinning. "Well, you can't go wrong seeing a woman who works at city hall. She's not bad looking, either with her bright red hair," he mumbled, shoving a cookie in his mouth.

"Oh, no, not me. I'm not looking to get married."

"Between Jenny and Karrie, you'd better watch out."

"And Jana Ann, my realtor," Quaid added. "Why do women always think men need to be married?"

"I don't know. It must be in their genes. I guess they don't think we can take care of ourselves. Alright, out with it, something's bothering you, what is it?"

Quaid ducked his head and leaned over in his chair, twisting his hands together. "I've been sitting here wondering about my life."

"I know things have been tough."

"You know I had one man think I was a drug addict because I shook and he wouldn't buy a painting from me. I also had a woman in a very nice restaurant told the manager that they shouldn't allow people like me in the restaurant, because I kept dropping my food off my fork and I spilled some of my wine."

"But, you can't keep hiding from people."

"I don't know what to do, I can't be around people, and I'll never paint like I did."

"Well, you need to take some time, you'll figure it out. I sure don't care if you shake and Daddy doesn't either. But there's more than your tremors bothering you."

"My birthday has made me think of my what ifs in my life."

"Yep, I understand. You know I wondered what life would have been like if I'd gone on to school. You know, I did have my scholarship to the university. Maybe then, I would have been better at business and owned a fleet of fishing boats, not just Daddy's one old boat. Of course," Levi's head swayed, "things might not have worked out for me and Jenny. Someone else might have snatched her up. Then what would my life have been like?"

"Like mine," Quaid said with remorse, rubbing his hands together.

"Well, would of and should of doesn't do us a hill of beans," Levi insisted, picking up another chocolate chip cookie from the plate. "Boy, these are good," he said, waving the cookie in the air.

Quaid stared at his old friend, Levi Sanders. They'd known each other most of their lives, Quaid growing up in New York and Levi growing up here in Hathaway Cove. They only saw each other once most years, a few times twice a year, when the Witherspoon family would vacation in the small town. The boys had become close over the years, so opposite of each other. Maybe that was the reason their friendship worked.

"Have you heard from Kevin?"

"Yep, we got a letter from him yesterday. He's coming home soon." Levi's anxious eyes peered over at his old friend. "We don't know when, but it can't be soon enough. It's driving Jenny crazy with worry listening to the news and she heard the army is sending more troops to Lebanon."

Quaid sighed and his lips tightened.

"Oh, I almost forgot," Levi said, laughing. "I guess I got carried away with the cookies. Jenny is going to Braelyn's tomorrow to be with her when the baby's born. I'll be a bachelor like you for a while. That's why she couldn't come over here today. She's packing and cooking for me. She said to tell you happy birthday and give you a hug, but I'll let her hug you herself the next time she sees you."

"I'll wait for my hug from her," Quaid replied, shaking his head. "A grandbaby? You're not going with her?"

"Nope, I'll let Jeff take over. He's one of the modern fathers. He'll change diapers, not me. I'd get in the way. Jenny's cooking me some meals so you can come over and eat good for a while. Unless you're too busy with Karrie or Jana Ann," he snickered, taking another bite from his cookie. He mumbled, "at least they can cook."

35

Ignoring Levi, Quaid slowly unwrapped his gift. "Alright," he announced, pulling out a large book, "The history of Hathaway Cove. Look at all these pictures." He held the book tight in his hands. "That Jenny sure is something…this is perfect."

"She knows you very well. Of course she should after all these years." Levi leaned forward in the overstuffed chair. "Oh, I see…now I understand," Levi paused, looking over at Quaid. "You're wondering about the other person who knew you even better than Jenny."

"Yes," Quaid answered. He laid the book on the table by his mug. "What if I hadn't been so stubborn and listened to my father? What would my life be like now if I'd have stayed here with Sandy like I wanted? What if I hadn't gone back to New York and married Karen?"

"I don't know, Quaid. I just don't know," Levi replied with sympathy in his voice, peering down at the floor. "We all have remorse, some small…others huge."

"I know," Quaid said, his eyes downcast looking at his trembling hands.

"One thing," Levi questioned, wiggling his head. His eyes peered up at the painting hanging over the fireplace.

"What?"

"That painting has something to do with you, doesn't it?" Levi questioned. "It has some mystery about it?"

"Yes, it does."

"Well," Levi asked. His head cocked to the side his eyes squinted, "are you going to tell me?"

"I painted that many years ago. It's a painting of Turtle Island."

"I knew it," Levi shouted, slapping his leg with his hand.

"I worked on the painting that entire summer and right before I left, I gave it to Sandy. I didn't sign it in the normal spot, because her mother would have known it was from me. She never liked me. She believed I was just using Sandy."

"I remember," Levi, moaned. "She did everything she could to break you two up. I think it made you both more determined to be together."

Quaid sighed, nodding his head yes.

"Alright, then why was the painting left here? It's an expensive painting, right?" Levi questioned.

"Yes, the painting is worth a lot of money. No one except Sandy, and now you, knows I painted it. I've been wondering the same thing. How and why did the painting end up here in this old cottage?"

"It's a mystery to me, an odd one that's for sure. It's what's driving you. Seeing the painting again. It's making you wonder about her?"

"I'm just curious of why the painting ended up here. Sandy hasn't lived in Hathaway Cove in years."

"You've been trying to find her, haven't you?" Levi took in a deep breath, his eyes still on the painting.

"I've done some inquiring. And I asked Jana Ann about the history of the cottage. It's no big deal," Quaid replied, staring down at his trembling hands.

"You know Sandy might not even be alive now. It's been a long time. Or maybe she's married with a slew of kids, maybe even grandchildren. I haven't seen her in years." Levi sat back in his chair, taking a sip of his soda, doing a slow swallow.

"I've thought a lot about what my life would have been like if I hadn't left her like I did," Quaid replied, clenching and unclenching his hands.

"Sometimes knowing is worse, but I'll keep my ear to the ground for any news. She's been gone a long time."

"Yes," Quaid answered, his eyes fixed on the last log burning in the fireplace. "It seems as if she just disappeared."

"I understand how you feel and I can see you ain't giving up searching for her."

37

"I have to have some closure. I don't know," Quaid ducked his head.

"If it's right then you'll find out something," Levi replied, grabbing one more cookie as he stood. "I better be getting home. I have some chores to work on around the house, since the weather's too bad to take anyone out fishing today." He chuckled. "I might have to run by and get Daddy and free him from Mama."

Amos would like you to come by. I know he doesn't like to stay cooped up in the house. Tell Jenny thanks for the book." Quaid followed Levi to the door. "I'll enjoy sitting by the fire studying the pictures."

"I sure will and I'll stop by when I'm a free man and bring some food."

Levi sipped the last of his soda, handing Quaid the can. He covered his head with the hood of his jacket before hurrying out in the rain to his old truck.

The front door closed. Quaid shivered feeling the cold air. He sat down in his comfortable chair and picked up one more cookie, as he slowly finished his cup of tea.

Quaid's phone began to ring as call after call came in from friends wishing him a happy birthday. The flames of the fire danced and his mind drifted from the conversations at hand. He wasn't really listening as they tried to persuade him to move back to New York. His friends believed he'd gone crazy wanting to live in an old worn out cottage on the beach. To leave his life of thirty years was insane in their opinion.

Maybe he was slowly going insane and he'd become one of those old men that kids made-up stories about. The one living in the dilapidated house at the end of the road with its sagging porch and windows framed with black shutters drooping like broken glasses. A haunted house with a wild haired man sitting by the window, staring out at them. He laughed touching his wild hair that was sticking out everywhere as he stared out the front window.

A Faded Cottage

The wind whistled around the cottage sending sheets of rain hitting the windows and roof. The cottage moaned, holding its own in the storm just as it had done so many times before as the tail of the storm crept on. Storms had a way of cleansing the world, maybe even cleansing the soul. Tomorrow would be a new day.

Quaid scooted to the edge of his chair watching the flames eat the log. Maybe Levi was right. Stirring up the past might not be a good thing. Maybe sometimes the past needed to stay buried. Ghosts can cause a lot of problems.

DIANN SHADDOX

A Faded Cottage

A Journey Home

Sandy's eyes stayed fixed on the road but her mind was on Quaid. Cars zoomed past as if her car was standing still. She felt as if she was in a fog and her foot wouldn't push down on the gas pedal. Her hands gripped the stirring wheel tighter and tighter. Her mind kept telling her to turn the car around go back to her condo where life was safe.

She looked in the rear-view mirror and her moist, green eyes peered back. No, she wasn't letting her mind win this time. For the first time in her life, she was thinking with her heart, hoping she wasn't going to get it shattered again. Her foot pushed down on the gas pedal letting the tall, South Carolina pines guarding Interstate 26 swish past.

Rain pelted the car, thunder boomed and lightning flashed as the wind whistled around the car, with the storm coming right at her. She laughed. Anyone seeing her now would think she was crazy, a mad woman alone in a car laughing out loud, holding onto the steering wheel as if it was about to fly out the window.

"No," she yelled, gripping the steering wheel even tighter. "You aren't winning." She'd been fighting fate for far too long. She wasn't giving up now.

She pushed the button on the CD player and their song from thirty years ago began to play. Her voice joined in and her worries faded. She smiled as the windshield wipers, swishing back and forth, began keeping time with the music.

The exit arrived. The car stopped at the stop sign. This was her chance to turn around and head home. It would be easy. Which way? Turn back on Interstate 26, or turn to the right—toward the small town. Her fingers wiggled on the steering wheel, turning it to the right. This was her one chance to find her answers.

The thunder boomed sounding like huge cannons firing from ships as the powerful storm continued marching onto land like a mighty warrior.

Sandy drove along the winding country road full of farmhouses with tattered barns dotting the landscape. Dogs lay sleeping under old drooping porches and the moss covered trees swayed from side to side in the fury of the storm. Old plantation homes that once ruled the land sat weathered and neglected with their fields of dried cotton covering their grounds.

A tear ran down her face. Time wasn't on her side. It was something she'd taken for granted in her life, such a precious thing...time. Sandy had always been a positive thinker but the last few years were weighing on her. Her head shook no. She wasn't wasting what time she had left in this world with worry and regret. She was going to live each day, every moment, to its fullest.

The car slowed as she drove across the coastal bridge, turning onto Main Street, leading her into the small seaside town. A weathered sign with faded blue letters announced Hathaway Cove and welcomed all of its visitors. The charming town sitting in the middle of an island surrounded by backwater and the Atlantic Ocean had only changed slightly in the last hundred years by the adding of electricity and running water. Generation after generation lived in the same homes with most of the people being fishermen just as their fathers and grandfathers before them, hardworking people.

Sandy's heart did a leap seeing the waves full of fury and power battling the shoreline. Her car window rolled down a tiny bit, the coolness of the sea air mingled with the sprinkles of rain made her tired body shiver. She took a deep breath pulling in the moist, sweet air of the ocean.

Magnolia Trees and short, squatty live oaks with huge branches draped in Spanish moss along with flowering red and pink camellia bushes framed the old historic homes along Main Street.

Sandy knew better but it didn't stop her. Her car turned down Front Street going to 817 Front Street. She drove passed her mother's small home, bringing back memories, some good, but many sad. Her mother struggled working two jobs and long hours just so Sandy would have a decent life and be able to go to college. She understood more of her mother's resentfulness of the Witherspoon family, especially Quaid. The tiny home sat quiet and the once massive oaks that stood guard in the front yard were now gone, merely a memory, just like parts of her life.

She sucked in a deep breath. One summer had changed her life. Now her past was drawing her back. She parked alongside the beach facing the massive ocean and rolled the window down. The salt air stung her face. This is where she belonged. The sea had drawn her in before and now the sea wouldn't let her go. She was home.

DIANN SHADDOX

A Faded Cottage

The Same Boat

Quaid watched the last log burn in the fireplace until it disappeared leaving glowing ashes.

The front door swung open, the cold wind hit his face. He hurried to the firewood stacked along the front wall of the porch pulling out a seasoned log. He carefully placed the log on top of the smoldering ashes in the hearth. Sparks flew. The flames began to consume the newly place log sending warmth into the chilly room.

Levi's visit had stirred up even more thinking.

Quaid, a boy of privileged upbringing, had grown up in Manhattan. He went to private schools, dressed in the best clothes, and was the most popular boy in his class. He belonged to the finest country clubs, and had his life laid out for him perfectly. He was supposed to marry the right girl and take over the prosperous family company from his father, McKinley Witherspoon, since he was the first-born son, but it wasn't his destiny. His brother, Bradley, and his son, Chandler, would run the family company, not his father's or grandfather Witherspoon's wishes.

Quaid failed many times to please his father and grandfather, but it didn't matter because he only dreamed of holding a paintbrush in his hand. Then, the unimaginable happened and he couldn't continue to paint. His world of art shows had spun to a stop, leaving him alone in his quiet condo.

The hardest part took place a year ago, when the long talks with his mom ceased. An evil had taken over her body. Dementia. Her once quick-witted mind had deteriorated, mixing up her memories from the past. Louise, a kind, energetic woman, was Quaid's greatest supporter, guiding him from a young age, never letting him down. The most optimist woman he had ever known had grown silent.

The day before he left for Hathaway Cove, Quaid sat down beside his mother, a beautiful woman with so much zest for life. She gently patted him on his hand as they talked. Then she took his hands in hers caressing them, looking into her son's eyes, not having to say anything, remembering for a few minutes. She was the only person in his life who understood what he was going through. How cruel life had become for them, taking away what they both loved, jumbling her memories, taking away his painting. He gave her a hug and tears ran down her soft, beautiful face. She knew she might not remember him visiting.

Why had his life changed? Until a couple of years ago, he believed he had everything any man would ever want, but did he? His mind wondered back to a peaceful time so long ago. He was painting right on this same beach with Sandy sleeping on her beach towel next to him. Soft sighs whispered in the air. Time would go by and she would wake. Her arms would stretch out wide and her long legs would run into the water, splashing the cool water over her heated body. His eyes would take in her every movement. His life was perfect for one summer when both of his loves sat right by his side. Tears began to flow down his face. Losing one love was difficult. Losing both was devastating.

A Faded Cottage

The old mantel clock over the fireplace began to chime, striking twelve, time for lunch. The pantry door swung open, he made his choice picking out a can of chicken noodle soup along with some crackers.

A noise startled Quaid. His chair scooted back from the table hurrying to the kitchen door. The porch light flicked on in the darkness of the storm. A light whimper came from the side of the porch. The wooden door swung open. Quaid leaned his head outside into the cool, damp air. There, next to the rocker snuggled close to the wall lay an old golden retriever, its light colored face staring up at Quaid with sad, brown eyes. Soaked from the rain, the dog's fur dripped onto the planks of the porch and its body shook as if he was waiting for someone to chase him away.

"Looks like you're cold and hungry," Quaid called out, but the dog didn't move. Quaid let the screen door close as he went to the refrigerator.

Quaid reached into the bottom cabinet pulling out an old tin pan and a small bowl. His elbow pushed open the screen door, setting the food and water on the porch floor. The dog lay on the porch, not taking his eyes off of Quaid.

"Look, you might as well eat. I'm not going to run you off. It looks like we're in the same boat. Granted it's not much," he said with a sigh. "It's listing to the side a little, huh?"

Drinking his soup, which was a lot easier than using a spoon, Quaid sat quietly at the table. The lid snapped on the tin of crackers and he picked up his empty bowl. He turned from the sink to go back to the living room, but stopped, curiosity was getting to him. He pulled open the kitchen door peering out onto the porch. The dog's brown eyes looked up contemplating Quaid's move and then the dog took another bite of fish from the tin pan.

"Not bad, is it?" Quaid assured. "Amos brings me some good fish. I'm glad you like it."

The screen door stayed ajar. Quaid hurried to the laundry room, grabbing an old towel from the top shelf to place on the porch for the dog to lie on. A noise startled him.

Quaid spun around and laughed. "Well come on in, boy. I guess we aren't standing on formalities. You might as well come in for a while and warm up."

The back door locked and Quaid switched the light off in the kitchen, going into the living room. The tired dog swirled in a half circle, lying down on the woven rug by the fireplace.

"I wonder what your name is? What did you do with your collar? Let's see." Quaid studied the old dog. "You need something different, a name to fit your personality." Quaid leaned against his chair. He smiled. "Rembrandt, yes, that fits you. You have a face Rembrandt would have loved to paint. The dog's head sank to the rug and his eyelids closed.

Leaning back in his overstuffed chair, calm settled over Quaid. Quaid picked up his new book, but his eyes kept going back to Rembrandt. He smiled. His friends would surely think he'd gone mad.

A Faded Cottage

The Dishes

The shadows from the flames flickered on the walls as time passed. Rembrandt yawned, making little yapping sounds breaking up the silence in the room before stretching and falling back to sleep. Quaid sat in his chair studying the pictures in his new book.

A car crunched the gravel in the driveway and he pulled himself out of the chair believing Levi had come back.

He unlocked the front door, opening it wide. He stood shocked. Standing in front of him was a petite woman holding a heavy tray of food balanced in her hands.

"Jana Ann, let me help you," he said quickly, taking the tray from the small woman.

"I made a beef roast this morning and it cooks better if it's large. I can't eat the entire thing so I thought maybe you might like some," the blonde, curly-haired woman explained, following Quaid into the kitchen.

"It smells delicious," he said trying to hold tight to the tray so it wouldn't shake, but the dishes continued to clank the entire way to the kitchen. He sat the large tray on the kitchen table. Quaid's eyes looked up at the round clock in the kitchen seeing it was five thirty, knowing Jana Ann would be glad to stay and eat dinner with him. It was a little over and above the call of duty for a realtor.

"I had a big lunch but I'll enjoy this later. Would you like a cup of tea or maybe a glass of chardonnay?"

"A glass of wine sounds nice," Jana Ann replied, moving close to him, making him nervous.

Quaid turned around keeping his back to her trying to hide his trembling hands. A chilled bottle of chardonnay pulled from the refrigerator. He gripped the wine bottle tightly in his hands, unscrewing the cork. The cork popped. For the moment, peering eyes stayed away. He carefully began to pour the liquid into the wineglass. His heart started pounding. The wine splashed, soaking into the placemat.

"It's so remarkable watching the waves," Jana Ann announced, staring out the window.

"This storm has been a doozy," Quaid assured, grabbing a towel as he cleaned up his mess.

Jana Ann let the blue curtain fall against the window of the door. She reached over lifting the glass of wine from the kitchen table not noticing the wet placemat. The tapping of her shoes trailed behind him as they made their way into the living room.

"The fire's nice." She paused for a moment next to the cracking flames. "It takes the chill out of the room." She turned from the fireplace, placing the glass of wine on the end table. "Oh, I didn't know you had a dog?" she gasped, staring down at the wet dog.

"Actually, I don't. Rembrandt here stopped by to visit for a while and I think he got tired of the cold."

"I don't blame him." Her hand reached into a long, skinny bag, and a few papers slid out. "I found out some information about the owners of this cottage."

He reached over, taking the papers.

"Thank you."

His reading glasses lifted from the table slipping them on his face. He gripped the pages tightly so they wouldn't flutter and slowly the pages flipped reading page after page.

"It seems Maggie Hendry, a realtor, bought this place from a Franklin Jackson a few years ago. She rented it during the time she lived here in town, but then she moved down to Miami. After her move, she decided to sell the cottage. She's on vacation until the middle of January so I can't get in touch with her. I couldn't find very much information on Franklin Jackson and I assume he was the one to buy the cottage from the Brookshire estate."

"It's not a big deal, Jana Ann. I was just curious," Quaid answered, staring up at the painting.

"We'll find out more when we talk to Maggie." Jana Ann took a breath. "Oh! I don't want to forget. I also wanted to invite you to spend Christmas day with me. I have a few friends who come around two o'clock and we all blend a mixture of food. We have a great time, share a little eggnog and wine. It's not formal, just a few old friends getting together. You don't have to bring anything."

"Sounds nice, I'll see. I haven't made any plans yet," Quaid replied quietly, knowing he wouldn't be going.

"I don't know about Rembrandt coming along," Jana Ann offered. Her eyes lowered, staring at the dog with her face all scrunched up. "I have a cat with an attitude and he doesn't get along with dogs."

"Rembrandt is only visiting. He might not be around long," Quaid chuckled, watching Jana Ann's face grow into a deeper frown.

"I guess I'd better get going," she said, taking the last sip of wine from her glass. "I'll stop by later on to pick up the dishes. You can let me know about your Christmas plans."

"Thank you for the invite."

Quaid stood from his chair but the small woman didn't move which left her standing way too close. This was getting awkward. He scooted past her to the front door.

"Thanks for the roast and for the information on the cottage. I'll let you know about Christmas Day."

"You're welcome, Quaid. I hope you will join us," Jana Ann urged. She stepped out the door onto the front porch. Her hood pulled up over her blonde hair before hurrying down the steps to her Mercedes.

A Faded Cottage
A Lifetime Ago

The dark storm clouds were unrelenting with swirling winds and heavy rain pounding the car. Sandy sat back in the driver's seat and tears rushed down her face as she listened to their old song play repeatedly, haunting her.

Why had fate brought him back into her life now? A time when her life was in turmoil much like the storm battering her car. She hadn't told anyone what she was doing, she knew her friends wouldn't understand and would have tried to stop her.

As a result, here she sat in the middle of a raging storm wondering if she had the courage to face Quaid and get her answers.

Her eyes stared out into the darkness letting memories swarm her mind. All of sudden, she could feel the warmth of the sun touching her skin. The waves danced on the shore and the seagulls squawked. She was asleep lying on the warm sand, and the ocean was serenading her. She woke hearing a voice. She looked up seeing those blues eyes staring down on her, eyes that have stayed with her for thirty years never leaving her mind.

Sandy smiled and her hands gripped the steering wheel. The car motor started and she drove through the small town, Hathaway Cove turning and going down Gull Lane.

****

Quaid closed the front door.

"Hey Rembrandt, it looks like we're eating fancy tonight."

He carefully unloaded the dishes trying to control his hands and placed the empty tray on a table near the front door. He lifted the lid off of one of the dishes and it clanked against the porcelain bowl. Anger grew as he examined the dish, seeing it was fine. He had become a child needing to use plastic dishes and plastic glasses all the time.

He began to relax. The mouthwatering smell of home cooking filled the room as he scooped some roast, chunks of potatoes, carrots, and onion along with brown gravy onto his plate. The full bowl of fruit salad told him this wasn't leftover from a meal, but something special Jana Ann cooked hoping to enjoy it with him.

The butter melted on his warm roll.

He laughed. A nudge of a wet nose hit Quaid's leg.

"I haven't forgotten you boy," he assured the dog, taking a chunk of roast and shredding it into Rembrandt's bowl. "Not bad, see? You hit the jackpot coming by today."

Rembrandt's head bent down as he slurped up the gravy.

"I see what you mean, she sure can cook."

The dog's brown eyes stared up in a wondering look.

"But remember, she has a cat and he doesn't like dogs."

The dog's big eyes continued to stare at Quaid as he tilted his head to the side.

Quaid chuckled. "You're right, at least we can eat well for a while."

Quaid sat at the kitchen table eating, thinking about the history of the cottage. If Franklin Jackson had bought this cottage from the family of Carlton Brookshire, Jr. and then he sold it to Maggie Hendry, what did they have to do with Sandy or the painting?

Quaid finished the last bite of his delicious meal snugging his back tight against his chair. He stared down at Rembrandt. "It was nice to have someone to share a meal with. Now we need to clean up this mess," he said, picking up his plate as Rembrandt ran to the back door.

"Alright," Quaid laughed. "I guess that's one way to get out of cleaning up the dishes."

Quaid's mouth clinched tight when his plate bumped the side of the sink leaving a huge chip. He pitched the plate into the trash can. *Well one less dish to clean*, he said to himself, becoming irritated seeing his hands as they shook uncontrollably. When the clinking dishes were finally stacked into the dishwasher, he rubbed his hands together knowing he'd been able to hide them from Jana Ann, but it was getting harder to do.

Wiping his hands on the dishtowel, Quaid wondered if his dinner guest had gone home. He stepped out the kitchen door onto the porch. He stood by the porch's railing mesmerized watching the invigorating storm. Thunder boomed, rumbling, shaking the cottage, echoing out to sea sending flashes of lightning that twirled across the water in a ballet show, arousing the swirling clouds. He thought of all the tales of pirate ships he'd heard over the years. Quaid laughed. Maybe he should buy a boat, set sail, and see what adventure he could find. The fish wouldn't care if his hands shook.

Rembrandt raced passed him running to his special spot in the living room, circling around and lying down on the old rug by the fireplace.

Quaid balanced a glass of wine in both hands as he cautiously moved into the living room. The wine he'd hoped would slow down the tremors for a while, even though living alone no one would notice his tremors but him. He sat back in his chair letting time tick by. The shadows from the flickering flames lit the dark room leaving peacefulness in their wake.

He lifted the glass of red wine to his lips and the wine splashed, splattering on his shirt. He tightened his grip on the stem of the glass, hurrying to the kitchen but it was useless and the glass crashed into the sink. Nothing was helping slow the tremors.

His hands laced together very tightly as the rage grew inside of him. "Why God?" He questioned. "Why me?" His hands raised in the air, his body full of anger.

Rembrandt nudged his nose against Quaid's leg.

Quaid smiled and his hands unlaced so he could gently rub the dog's soft fur. "I guess life isn't fair for many of us, is it boy?"

After the mess in the kitchen was cleaned and his shirt changed, Quaid sat down in his chair. Once more, he held a glass of wine in his hand and took a sip, letting the liquid flow down his throat. He tightened his grip on the stem of the glass, resting it on the arm of the chair.

"This has been some birthday, Rembrandt. Most people would think I should be the happiest man in the world. You don't know this, but I've made a name for myself in the art world. It took many, many years of hard work, but I've painted hundreds of pieces. I was even able to meet Ronald and Nancy Reagan, a memory I won't ever forget.

See," Quaid began quietly, cupping his hands together, letting them sway in slow rhythm. "Back when I was young, five years old, I started drawing and scribbling on everything, even things I shouldn't," he chuckled, "until my mom bought me my first art set. It was full of pencils, paints of every color, along with gleaming white paper. It didn't take long for my small hands to bring the sea to life on pieces of paper, then canvas.

My mother was thrilled. She sent me to this old grumpy man named Kerrigan. I guess now I understand him more. The first thing he did was to have me draw, on my own, not telling me what to draw.

A Faded Cottage

He sat there in his worn high back chair, twisting his long mustache, staring at me. Each class continued with the same piece of art I'd started in the beginning. I added to the painting each visit, time after time. He never commented about what I'd drawn. Then he began teaching me techniques. At the end of the school year, he held up my painting, the one I'd added to from the beginning. He smiled for the first time."

"Son, this piece tells your story, not only what you see and how much passion you have in your paintings, but the course of learning something new from each class. You can tell where you've grown. Each stroke has become defined over the year. Now you're ready to find your own niche. Never second-guess your work. Stay true to your art."

"I guess the old man died years ago. You know I never went back to thank him," Quaid said overwhelmed. "I should have."

****

Sandy slid the car to a quick stop on the side of the road. 11 Gull Lane was a few houses down. A soft light glowed in the window of the living room and smoke twirled from the old brick chimney.

She sat quietly, collecting her thoughts. Her moist eyes peered back at her from the rearview mirror and her hands gripped the steering wheel. Her head shook, no. He wouldn't see tears, not today. She'd stay the night with KC. Tomorrow would be soon enough.

A smile came on her face. She wasn't going to let her mother win, not this time, she was going to walk into the cottage and show Quaid what he had missed all these years.

DIANN SHADDOX

A Faded Cottage

A New Day

The clock chimed eleven. He looked down at Rembrandt. "I'm getting tired and I reckon," Quaid laugh trying to use his southern voice. "I'd better let you outside for a while."

Quaid's arms wrapped around the post of the porch. The dark rain clouds were moving on and the moon's rays were peeping out between the last of the clouds, casting shadows over the water.

Rembrandt ran down the porch steps.

The cool night air touched Quaid's face and his eyes closed. He took in a deep breath of salt air. This was his life, not his past, not a bad life.

Rembrandt patiently waited at the door.

Quaid turned around.

The dog nudged the wooden door with his nose, hurrying inside.

"Sorry Rembrandt, I don't have a special bed for you but the rug is nice," Quaid assured, turning the quilt down on the bed. "At least it's a lot dryer and warmer than being outside."

Quaid unzipped his jeans, slipped them off, and hung them on the back of a chair. The lamp clicked off, turning the room dark. Quaid slipped under the quilt, pulling it up around his neck. He was tired from too much thinking. His head swished deep in the feather pillow, whispering in the quiet room, "Happy Birthday, Quaid."

Quaid woke up at seven just as he had each day since he had moved into the cottage. He sat up in bed. Rembrandt was sound asleep, his body softly moving with each breath, lying on the quilt across the foot of the bed. So much for getting a dog bed. Quaid carefully lifted the quilt trying to slip out of the bed, but the old dog's head lifted as he watched him.

"Good morning. I see you slept well," Quaid chuckled, going around the bed to the bathroom.

Rembrandt scrambled in a hurry, jumping off the bed.

Quaid grabbed his old jeans from the back of the chair, slipping them on, pulling out a clean sweatshirt from the drawer of the chest, and hurried to the kitchen for his first cup of coffee.

Rembrandt stood patiently by the kitchen door until it swung open, letting the dog push the screen open, running outside into the early morning.

"Oh this is nice," Quaid said, stepping onto the porch, holding tight to his cup of coffee. "I love watching the sun rise after a storm."

It was a beautiful December day and the old metal thermometer hanging on one of the porch's post said forty-seven degrees. Quaid knew the warm sun would bring the temperature up quickly reaching the high sixties.

The old rocker creaked and Quaid tightened his lips seeing the colors bursting in the sky with such magic. The morning sun sparkled on the water as it raised high in the sky. He wanted to grab a paintbrush, letting his hands begin, but he couldn't...not anymore. He took in a deep breath, gripping the arm of the chair with his hands clinched tight. Why had his hands abandoned him?

The rocker stopped. "Enough of feeling sorry for myself. Let's go see if ole Amos is out fishing."

His sweatshirt jacket zipped making the layers of clothes bulky. The old boards creaked as he stepped on the boardwalk crossing the sand dunes moving by habit down to the water's edge, kicking at the sand, sending grains up into the moist air. The wind picked the fine granular specks scattering them over the water like the sands of time, vanishing into the sea. Dark waves viciously licked at his shoes with each step, trying to catch him off guard.

Rembrandt ran past him out to the ocean's edge and played with the water, letting the cold spray try to catch him, missing each chance of getting wet with experience in teasing the waves. A lone seagull swooped down near Quaid's head, squawking, fussing at him for not having any food.

The sun was beginning to warm the day. Quaid meandered along the edge of the water but before he rounded the one curve on the beach, he stopped and his eyes closed. His mind replayed the warm summer day he spent right at this exact spot when he was eighteen. It was their first meeting and the one he wouldn't forget. It would stay in his mind forever. He could see the beautiful girl lying right in front of him. The lone seagull flew over his head squawking, bringing his thoughts back from the past.

He smiled again. Down at the end of the beach was ole Amos. Life was as it should be.

Amos Sanders owned his own fishing boat, a small company named Sanders Fishing Expedition, for over fifty years. He retired last year leaving his operation to his son, Levi. Amos taught Quaid everything about fishing along the South Carolina coast. After Quaid moved to the cottage, he spent most of his mornings fishing and talking with Amos. Talking seemed to help both Amos and Quaid adjust to their new lives.

"Good morning, Quaid. Happy birthday," the old man called out. "Awe, don't be so surprised. Levi told me. Sorry I missed you yesterday morning, but Georgina wouldn't let me out of the house. She said it was too damp and cold."

"Well she was right. How's the fishing today?"

"I've already caught a few. The storm stirred up the fish, confusing them," Amos said, bending over near the dog standing by him. "Who's this?"

"This is Rembrandt. I thought you might know him."

"Nope, I haven't seen him around before. Nice to meet you Rembrandt," the old man said, petting the dog's head. "You told him I might give him a fish. I see it in his face." Amos chuckled. "Now, have a seat and tell me what is bothering you," he declared, never one to beat around the bush.

The small folding stool popped open and Quaid sat down. "I guess it's turning fifty. I don't know."

Quaid's eyes squinted in the bright sunlight looking at the seventy five year old man with wrinkles on his cracked face from years out in the sun aboard his fishing boat.

Amos grinned back a Quaid. "Son, life isn't so bad. You still have a lot of living to do. I understand this hasn't been a good year, but you get out of life what you put into it. It was hard on me to give up my boat, knowing I couldn't handle her anymore." He wiggled his fishing pole. "But sitting out here fishing is just as rewarding. Circumstances change, but you take those old lemons and squeeze them and you make you some mighty fine lemonade."

"It's…" Quaid began as he shook his head to the side. "My past keeps coming at me, jumbling up my mind. I don't know what my future is."

"Yep, it's a funny thing about memories; they can become reality, if you don't watch yourself." Amos's bushy eyebrows rose. "Now, don't let the past or the future worry you. Live in the present. You'll be fine; don't let life get to you."

Quaid shook his head, trying to understand.

Amos grinned with the same grin of Levi. "I heard the women are after you," Amos declared with a twinkle in his eye. "You sure are making a stir around these parts. We ain't had a bachelor around in a while."

"I know, they keep bringing me food," Quaid laughed. "At least I'm going to be eating well for a while."

"Son," the old man chuckled, "don't underestimate those women. They'll have you hogtied before you know what's happening. They'll straighten your life out whether you want them to or not." He pulled his line in. "You want to fish for a while? I brought my other fishing rod. It's back there along with the lures and some bait. You do whatever you like."

"Sure," Quaid answered, getting up from the stool. He gripped the fishing rod watching his line out in the water, not worrying if his hands were trembling. He was safe from prying eyes, ole Amos and Rembrandt didn't care what his hands were doing.

"Well, it's getting late and Georgina will have lunch ready soon," Amos announced, lifting his fish into a small bucket. "Hey Rembrandt, you're a lucky dog. Fishing was good today." The old man leaned over, petting the dog.

Amos picked up his folding stools and fishing rods. "Now Quaid, life isn't that complicated, you need to take some time. Remember live one day at a time," Amos assured. "You'll see it'll work out fine. Worry is a waste of time and don't help anyone."

"Thanks for the talk and the fish. See you tomorrow."

"Yep, I heard the weather is going to be nice for a few days so I can get out of the house. Bye Rembrandt," Amos called out, walking over the dune. The dog barked and the old man waved goodbye.

Quaid thought about what Amos had said. He crossed the boardwalk going to the south side of the cottage, letting the fish slide from the bucket onto the cleaning table. He gripped his hands, trying to control them, pulling out the sharp knife. He'd learned long ago from Amos how to clean fish, but now he used his own technique that he'd come up with, the only way to control the knife with his quivering hand, and on most days, it worked and today seemed to be one of his good days.

"Hey Rembrandt, we're going to have some good fried fish tonight," Quaid declared, looking down at the dog. The mess of fish scraps, heads, and tails raked into a big pot sitting down by the bottom of the table. The lone seagull squawked, circling over Quaid's head, impatiently waiting for his treat. The water sprayed from the hose, rinsing off the table. He pushed open the wooden door, hurrying into the kitchen, the pan of clean fish slid in the refrigerator.

"Let's go back outside and sit on the porch," Quaid said, pushing the screen door open.

The wicker rocker crackled when he sat down. Quaid watched the seagull with some help from his friends finish the scraps of fish. Rembrandt spun around in a circle, and then he stretched out long, his eyes closed.

"The day sure is a lot nicer than yesterday. Maybe, Amos is right about life and I need to calm down and live each day and stop worrying about what could have been. I can't change the past."

The bright sun began to warm the porch as the rocker moved back and forth in a slow rhythm matching the waves swishing onto shore in a soothing tempo. His body heaved a sigh as Quaid closed his eyes. All in all, this wasn't a bad life.

Tires scrunching on the gravel out front brought him back from his thoughts. Quaid stood, leaning over the railing on the porch. "I'm out back," he called, hearing light footsteps. "Jana Ann, I'm sitting outback on the porch."

A woman walked around the corner of the cottage. She stopped.

Quaid's heart quit beating.

A Faded Cottage

Eyes from the Past

The woman's green eyes gazed at him as she stood by the corner of the cottage, letting her light brown hair blow in the gentle sea breeze. She finally began to walk, making her way around the edge of the porch to the steps.

His fingers smoothed his hair from his face as he rubbed his eyes. He moved in slow motion across the porch, stopping at the top of the steps.

Her fingers wrapped around the railing of the porch. She placed her foot on the bottom step. Her eyes never looked down; they were still on the eyes of the man standing at the top of the steps, the eyes from her past. She continued as if in slow motion moving up the steps. She stopped on the top step for a few seconds, facing the man with her ankles tight together not able to move. He backed up. Another step and there she stood only inches from the man, able to smell his cologne, feeling his body breathing, seeing the same boy of thirty years ago.

Her body froze in its spot as her eyes took him in. He was thicker in the middle with speckled grey in his generous dark hair, but his face was the same with those eyes, as deep blue as the water. Her mind spun, a jolt of panic taking over. What was she thinking, coming here without considering the consequences? Maybe that was the problem, she hadn't thought. She'd packed and drove.

Her hand continued to grip the porch railing trying to find some support as flashes of the past blurred before her eyes. She was back at this same cottage, a place that had pulled her in many times. She was standing on the porch where time and again she had sat reliving her past. Now her past was standing right in front of her.

She wiped her sweaty palms on her jeans. She'd tried to hide the dark circles under her eyes this morning putting on extra makeup, not wanting him to see she had been crying. A sharp breath of air filled her lungs. Standing in front of her was the only man she'd ever loved. She prayed this wasn't a mistake. She wanted answers but on the other hand, she didn't know if she could stand the pain. Her insides tingled feeling his eyes on her and she thought she might pass out.

"How are you doing, Quaid?" she finally spoke, breaking the silence.

"I'm doing pretty well, Sandy," Quaid said, his voice crackling with nervousness as he back away from her going to his rocker. His eyes told him she was really in front of him, so beautiful, so real, but his mind couldn't believe it. Was she a ghost?

He kept staring and Sandy finally laughed. "You still stare a lot, don't you?"

He laughed. His body throbbed with fervor wanting to reach over and grab her to see if she was flesh and blood, wondering if he was dreaming. "Would you like to have a seat?"

"Who's this?" Sandy asked turning away from Quaid.

"His name's Rembrandt. He's merely visiting," Quaid, answered

She squatted down, petting the old dog. "You need a bath, boy."

"Yes, he does, but since he's a visitor I decided to let it go."

"How long have you had him?"

"Just a day now."

"I see." She sat down in the other rocker and turned her face to Quaid. "You do like to stare a lot. It's not difficult to figure out, Jenny called a friend of mine, KC, and she told me you had moved here. I guess I was curious of you as you were of me. It's been a long time."

"Yes, I guess word got back to Jenny."

"You know Jenny, she believes in happy ever after," Sandy explained. The rocker moved slowly. "I haven't seen them in years. I've stayed way too busy." She knew it wasn't the complete truth, Jenny and Levi made her think of Quaid, bringing back to many painful memories.

He wanted to ask if happy ever after had worked for her, but he didn't. This was difficult and maybe the past shouldn't be brought up.

She turned her head towards the water, but she knew he was staring and wondering about her life as she was wondering about his. Jenny had said he wasn't married, but didn't tell if he was seeing someone else.

His eyes peered down staring at her left hand. She had a ring on her one finger, but was it a wedding ring, he couldn't tell.

"How's your mom doing?" he asked leaning over in his rocker gripping his hands.

"She died years ago. She got breast cancer when I was in college and died the year I graduated. She fought hard but," Sandy paused, staring down at the floor, "the fight was too much for her."

"I'm sorry to hear that. My mom has second stage dementia. She has some good days but lately there have been more bad ones."

"That's terrible. Your mom was always so kind to me. I always wished my mom was more carefree like her instead of being so judgmental."

"It's sad to see her not remembering the fun times, but it's amazing she still comes up with some interesting comments. Her mind is still thinking and her compassion for others is still there."

67

Sandy rested her head against the rocker and her eyes slowly closed. "It's so relaxing out here. I haven't been to the beach in years, and no, I don't wear a bikini anymore. But, I do like to go swimming and lay out in the sun," she added laughing.

He smiled; she was a blunt as always, a trait he did enjoy.

"KC has kept me informed of some things going around here. It's interesting how many things have stayed the same. This town doesn't change much," she added leaning her head against the rocker.

Quaid's head nodded. "It's been like stepping back in time."

He couldn't help himself; his eyes studied Sandy as she sat only a couple of feet away. He took all of her in. She was now a woman, not a girl anymore, sitting so confident. She hadn't changed a bit, the shape of her face and those eyes full of sparkle, knowing he had really stepped back in time.

Quietly they rocked for a while, thinking, wondering, and remembering.

His feet grabbed the porch floor and his hands wrenched together in a circle. "Would you like a glass of wine or something to drink?" He finally asked able to think clearly.

"A glass of wine would be nice."

"Is Cabernet alright? I do have some chardonnay in the refrigerator if you would like?"

"Red wine is fine." She wondered who the chardonnay was for, maybe Jana Ann, the name he had called out.

He stood from the rocker and Sandy took all of him in, every aspect of the man in front of her. The thick, dark hair, blue eyes the color of the sea and his smile that made her feel warm inside. Thoughts of their summer and what their lives could have been together washed over her, but the main question of why had he left her and hadn't come back lingered in her mind. She shook away the doubt. Good or bad, she wanted answers.

His hands gripped the screen door pulling the wooden door open. The sound of his shoes broke the silence that had fallen over the kitchen. Quaid lifted a glass from the cabinet gripping the bottle with both hands pouring the wine only filling the glass half way. He took a deep breath, terrified of handing the glass of wine to her, but before he could lift it from the counter, a hand reached around him.

"Thank you," she offered, lifting the glass from the counter standing so close she was able to feel his body breathing.

He shuddered when the green eyes peered into his eyes. Trying to get his composure, he nervously tried to think of words to break the silence. "I have some homemade cookies if you're hungry?"

Sandy gave him a confused look.

"No," he chuckled, "I didn't make them. A friend brought them over."

Her mind swirled again with questions. "No, thanks, the wine is fine." She smiled. "It's a little late but, happy birthday, Quaid," she said in a sensuous voice, lifting her glass in a toast.

"You remembered?"

"I remember everything," she answered. Her eyes turned from him. "You know," she said softly taking a sip of wine, "I owned this cottage many years ago. I spent many vacations here. I see not much has changed."

Now he was curious, who was Franklin Jackson, her husband? "You owned this cottage? Why didn't anyone around here know that?"

"I kept my visits quiet. It was a place to come and relax and hide away from everyone."

"I understand. It's a great place and I've enjoyed living here these past few months. There is serenity about this old faded cottage and it seems to welcome you in."

"Yes, there is. I used to stay here as much as I could, but somehow the place became sad. You've brought back the warmth the cottage used to have." She sighed. "I like its name – a faded cottage."

"I fell in love with this place the first time I saw it," he said in a quiet voice. "I had to live here when…" He continued to stare not able to finish his sentence.

Her fingers gripped tight the wine glass. "The painting is…" She stepped into the living room, "yes, I see the painting is still here." She smiled back at him, not saying anything else. The only other person who knew the secret of the painting and the answer to the mystery of why it was left here.

He stayed quiet, not asking his question, hurrying to the kitchen door.

Sandy stepped outside onto the porch and her body shivered.

Quaid turned back inside grabbing a small throw. "Here," he said gently, wrapping the throw around her shoulders. "It's getting cooler out."

"Thank you," she said. Her body tingled, but this time not from the chillness in the air. She could feel his breathing inches from her neck. She stepped away from him moving to the edge of the porch.

"I don't want to miss a minute sitting out on the porch," she said in a soft voice. Then she took in a nervous breath. "Have you been back?" The words came out before she could think. "Out there," she said softly, tilting her head to the side, using it as a pointer. "Since you moved back?" Her eyes studied the old boards on the floor, not able to look at Quaid. Why had she asked this question?

"No, I haven't," he answered, giving her a curious look as he leaned back in his rocker. His hands laced over his head, waiting for her response.

"Well, I'd love to go there unless you have someone who might not want us to do that."

"No one would care, but it's getting too late tonight."

"I'm staying at KC's. It's too much for me to drive back to Colombia tonight. How about we go in the morning?" She studied him, watching for a reaction. "I'm sure we can find a small boat."

His feet gripped the floor and the rocker stopped moving. "Alright, how about a picnic like we used to do?"

"Sounds like fun. I can stop by the deli on Main on my way over in the morning. You have the wine," she added eagerly. Her feet swished against the old planks of the porch. "It'll be fun to go back to the island."

"Don't get your hopes up. It might not be the same," Quaid cautioned. Could this be real, maybe his luck was changing.

"Do you mind taking a walk on the beach?"

"A walk sounds nice. What do you say, Rembrandt?"

The old dog stretched his front legs letting his body wiggle from his tail to his head.

Quaid's trembling hands tugged on the zipper of his jacket, pulling it tight around his neck.

Sandy rewrapped the throw around her shoulders. From habit, her feet moved down the steps off the porch onto the worn beach path, her shoulders tense, knowing he was watching her every move as he followed closely behind her.

A deep breath of air filled her lungs. "Oh, this is so nice. I've missed the crispiness of the salt air." Her body moved smoothly down to the beach alongside Quaid. With each step her breathing became calmer. Their footsteps crunched on the silky sand as the colorful evening sun made shadows across the deep grayish-blue water.

Quaid kicked the sand.

She laughed. "You still stir up the sand."

"I like watching it fly into the air." He stopped walking. "Sorry, I forgot you didn't like me kicking the sand, because it would stick to your legs."

"I have pants on today, so no problem. Oh, I do love it here," she said wrapping her arms tighter around her body. "I fell in love with the Low country when my mom and I first moved here. I miss living right on the beach. There's a peacefulness about the area. It has its own mystique."

71

They continued walking, taking slow steps. They rounded the curve. Sandy stopped walking. Her eyes looked up at him. "Do you remember how burned I was the first day we met? It was a good thing you said something to me. I did fall asleep, but I wasn't going to tell you. You stood there so full of yourself. I'd never met anyone like you before, so confident." She took in some air, not saying anything for a second, finally exhaling, hoping she wasn't saying too much. "I was cooked that day. Quaid," she paused, "you're staring again."

"I can't help it. It's a memory that won't go away," he added, shrugging his shoulders. "I guess I don't want it to. Sorry."

"No," she said, stepping close, putting her hand on his arm.

His body tensed.

"Please, never say you're sorry," she said in a soothing voice. "Regrets don't help us. I know. I've lived with many regrets for most of my life. It eats at your soul."

Sandy's gentle fingers continued to caress his arm. He wanted to tell her how sorry he was for leaving her and make the years disappear, but before he could think anymore, she let go of his arm. He stood there paralyzed not able to move.

She giggled.

His shoulders relaxed remembering her warm touch.

"Mom always believed I got sunburned because of you. She said I stayed out too long talking to you. She never did believe the real story that I had fallen asleep lying on the beach all alone."

"There were plenty of other times you got in trouble because of me."

"Remember when we came back to the marina from Turtle Island late Friday or," she giggled again, "early Saturday morning? We let time get away from us."

"I won't ever forget that night. We had everyone worried," he paused, "but we had fun. Until we got back to the marina. I'll always remember pulling the boat up to the dock and everyone, including Amos and my parents, standing looking down at us in the moonlight.

I tried to keep a straight-face but Amos kept winking at me with his stupid grin on his face."

"That's the time your father found out about us," she said softly, lowering her eyes to the sand. "He wasn't happy but your mom calmed him down, at least for the day."

Quaid looked out to the water, his mouth tight.

"Quaid, it's alright." Sandy reached over and squeezed his arm. "I knew your father didn't think I was good enough for you. He was only trying to look out for you. I understand that now." Sandy's head shook, no. "I wasn't from the upper crust of society. It was hard back then thinking he was right. It's why you left that summer without saying goodbye, isn't it?" She let go of his arm and took in a deep sigh. It had taken thirty years but she was finally able to ask her question.

His body spun around and he put his quivering hands on her shoulders. "You're wrong! I wanted to see you but I knew I wouldn't be able to leave you if I did. My dad didn't let me out of his sight the last couple of days we were here. I tried to sneak out the night before we left but he caught me climbing out the window."

"Okay then," she asked, her face puckered, "what aren't you telling me?"

Quaid's hands fell from her shoulders and he looked down toward the ground. "The morning my family left, Billy told me you were fine with me leaving and you already had a date with him and for me not to worry, he'd take care of you."

"You believed him?" She yelled in a high pitch scream. "Why would you ever believe that son of a bitch? Maybe you wanted to believe him to make it easier for you to leave."

"Nothing could have made it easier for me to leave you," Quaid said anxiously, letting his foot kick the sand. "I thought it was over between us when you didn't show up on the beach for our last date."

"My mom caught me before I left to meet you. She said you were using me and you'd go back to New York and I'd never hear from you again. She thought you were a spoiled, rich kid trying to get his way. I guess I bought into the story…" her voice trailed off and she became quiet.

"Oh Sandy, it wasn't like that at all, she was wrong," he declared, trying to defend himself, "but I guess my dad and your mother won. I moved on with my life and believed you wanted to do the same. Especially when I didn't hear back from you."

"Hear back from me?" she questioned with her voice squealing.

"Yes. I waited and waited to get your answer.

"Answer to what?" she questioned, her body quivering with anxiousness.

"Your answer to the question in the letter I sent. I told you how I felt but I never heard from you. I waited for weeks, checking the mail, praying for a reply. When I didn't hear anything…"

"I never got a letter from you. I waited, too, hoping to hear from you, thinking you'd call or write," she assured, "I even hoped you might show up. But nothing. I guess my mom intercepted the letter," she whispered, not finishing her sentence. Tears brimmed in her eyes and her throat tightened as the breath was sucked from her body with the realization he did love her. Their summer was real, but so many years had disappeared, so much time. A lifetime. Was their love still there?

"Remember, regrets won't help. Did you ever become a botanist?" he asked, quickly changing the subject.

"Yes, and I love my work," she answered, letting the past fade from her mind.

"You always loved plants."

"The plants along this coast are amazing. Each one has its own job to do. They're very important to us humans even though most people take them for granted. The grass plants here," her arms spread out wide as her body twirled in a circle, "help prevent erosion, or we wouldn't have such beautiful beaches. The plants and tree's affect our climate and our life filtering impurities from our air." Then she paused. "I'm going on too much. I'm doing it again."

"I recall your speeches. You do have a passion for plants."

"They're living things and should be cared for." Rembrandt's wet nose nudged her. "Yes, like you," she chuckled, leaning over petting the dog, his big eyes looking up at her. She shivered standing back up. "It's getting cold and I'm hungry. Rembrandt and I are having some fresh fish we caught with Amos this morning and I can cook some rice," Quaid offered, rubbing his trembling hands together. "You're welcome to join us if you'd like. I'm learning to cook so it's not half bad."

"Sounds good," Sandy answered, flipping sand in the air, letting it fly at him. She turned and ran with Rembrandt following her leaving Quaid standing on the beach staring.

Laughing, he ran, digging his feet into the soft sand racing down the beach to catch her.

An older couple about Amos's age, wrapped arm in arm strolled slowly coming at him. Quaid's pace slowed.

Good evening, it's a nice evening out," the short man with thinning grey hair offered.

"Yes, the evening is wonderful, everything is wonderful," Quaid called back to the couple, seeing Sandy way down the beach with Rembrandt at her side, waving her arms in the air.

Sandy stepped up on the porch and she picked up the two wine glasses sitting on the table.

Quaid opened the back door. Rembrandt pushed his way past them both, running to the living room.

"Alright," Quaid called out, following the dog, "we need a fire." He knelt down in front of the fireplace placing another log on the smoldering ashes. "The fire feels good doesn't it boy," he said slapping his hands together as the tiny pieces of dried bark fell to the floor. "The days are nice, but the evenings are a little cool."

Sandy folded and laid the throw on the back of the chair in the living room. Her fingers tightened on the chair's back as her eyes were pulled to a tray of nice dishes sitting on a small table near the front door, wondering who else had visited the small cottage.

Quaid stood back up, moving past Sandy going to the kitchen. "Come on, I need to start dinner," he said, excitedly waving his arm. He began to clean the fish laying each piece of fish on a platter patting them dry. The spices twirled in their container on the counter and generously he sprinkled a few of them over the fish. The pot full of water sat on the stove ready for the rice.

"How can I help?" Sandy questioned.

"The dishes are over there in the side cabinet," he motioned, pointing with his hand. "If you wouldn't mind setting the table," he said laughing. "I guess you already know where they are."

"No problem," Sandy assured, moving over to the small china cabinet. She placed the plates on the table along with the silverware and then she picked up her glass of wine taking a long slow sip. It was so different standing here in the cottage with him. Her mind flooded with memories, bringing back a passion she hadn't felt in years.

Sandy bought the cottage years ago during a difficult time in her life, a time when she needed to find peace. This cottage, Miss Eula's cottage on 11 Gull Lane, had pulled her in once; giving her the peace she needed. Now it had brought her back. She discreetly wiped a lone tear, not letting it fall down her face. Her hand gripped the back of the kitchen chair. She was tired from the day, and knew she was growing weak. The medicine wasn't working. Her head shook no as her hands tightly squeezed the chair. She wouldn't mess up this evening.

The fish sizzled in the hot pan.

"I hope this taste all right," he said.

"It'll be great," she said softly, bringing her thoughts back trying not to worry about what the future held.

"You know I'm learning how to cook."

"I guess it is very different for you without servants doing the cooking and cleaning."

He could hear the sarcasm in her voice. "Yes it is."

"I'm sorry, I didn't mean anything. You have lived such a different life than I have."

"I remember your mom calling me a spoiled rich kid, I guess she was right."

"Quaid…"

He interrupted. "I'm managing on my own," he said looking down at his hands as they tried to scoop the fish from the skillet, but the fish kept sliding from the spatula. "I told Rembrandt I was going to practice making shrimp," he added trying to change the subject. "I found a recipe I just might have to try it."

"Tomorrow we can get some shrimp from the marina and I'll show you how to cook them. Mom taught me how to cook a few things, not many, but shrimp was one," she added, placing napkins on the table. "I can also make a Lowcountry Boil but it makes up a lot of food for two people. I also have a great chowder recipe I can cook for you, too."

"Sounds good to me," Quaid assured. "Anytime you want to cook, no problem."

Quaid's body flexed. He couldn't pick up the fish from the skillet because his hands were shaking wildly. He turned his body away from her trying to hide his trembling hands, but before he could hide them, Sandy moved next to him.

He panicked.

Her body brushed close to his and she softly placed her hands on top of his hands with a gentle, stroking motion.

She nodded her head. "Sorry is a waste of time and your hands are fine," she whispered, looking up into his face.

He took a deep breath, fighting back tears. She knew his secret. Quaid looked down at her. "This is the reason I live alone. I can't stand being incompetent, a bungling idiot."

Her head shook yes, she understood. She picked up the spatula and her calm hand lifted the lightly fried fish onto a platter. She then scooped out the rice into a bowl setting the platter and bowl on the table.

He reached over and poured the wine into the glasses on the table not worried the wine was splashing out. Sandy sat there staring at him not his hands.

"I also have some fruit salad," he offered, going to the refrigerator and setting the bowl on the table, carefully lifting off the lid.

"The fish is delicious," she said, taking another bite. "You just may become a gourmet cook after all. You always did everything just so. Nothing was half ass for you."

"Not anymore," he quietly added looking at his trembling hands. He also knew he didn't do everything correctly; he had let her go.

Sandy sat back in the kitchen chair sipping her wine, looking around the room. He hadn't changed a thing.

"I can hear the waves," she said in a soft voice. Her head leaned against the slats of the chair and her hair fell down onto her back. "I've always loved listening to the rhythm of the waves." Her eyes closed. Her mind was fighting with her conscience, wanting to stay the night. But it wasn't right, not when there were too many unanswered questions.

"I don't think I'll ever get tired of the swishing of the waves," Quaid said. "The ocean pulls you into its secret world. I guess you're lucky when you become a part of it," he replied. His mind swirled. She was so beautiful. He wanted to forget all the protocol of life and grab her. *Get a grip Quaid*, he said silently in his mind, *give her some time*.

She shook her head yes, agreeing with him about the ocean, remembering how much he loved the waves.

He stood from the table and she started to move.

"I'll clean the kitchen, you're a guest," he said, picking up the dishes letting them clank together.

"I don't want to be a guest," Sandy answered. Standing, picking up her plate and moving toward the sink.

He rinsed the dishes and she loaded them into the dishwasher, and each dish made it without adding new chips.

"Don't forget, I have some cookies."

"The wine is fine," she assured, moving into the living room. Sandy gazed at the painting over the fireplace. She could see all of the painting's secrets hidden deep inside; secrets of love he had painted especially for her.

Quaid stood in the kitchen doorway taking in every inch of her.

Sandy could feel his stare, but she didn't look back. It was so comforting. Tears built in her eyes and her hand moved to her face, trying inconspicuously to wipe the wetness. It was so difficult to be this close to him after all these years.

Thoughts swirled in her head. She whispered, *if I had received his one letter, things...* Her head shook no. The past couldn't be fixed. She did wonder what the one letter said. However, she wasn't going to ask, not now, it would be too painful. She had to stay in control and not let the past control her.

"I hate to leave, but I need to get back to KC's. I shouldn't go in too late."

Sandy turned and leaned down next to Rembrandt "Goodbye boy, it was nice meeting you. She stood up. "I'll see you in the morning about eight thirty, if it's alright?"

"Eight thirty is fine. The weather's supposed to be nice, a little windy."

"I'll wear a sweatshirt with a hood and I'll be here early enough to help you get everything packed. See you in the morning," she said excitedly. "Oh," Sandy moved over to the table sitting next to the wall and grabbed a piece of paper and a pen from the drawer. "Here's KC's phone number in case you need it."

"Wait a minute," Quaid gestured, swinging his arm, picking up a card from the table.

"Brenton Quaid Witherspoon, artist," she read. "It still has a New York address on it."

"Yes, but I changed the phone number. I'm not moving back to New York."

"Good night, Quaid. I'll see you in the morning." Sandy stepped outside on the front porch. She didn't move for a second, a soft breeze of fresh cool air filling her lungs bringing her thoughts back to the present.

"Good night, Sandy." The words exited his mouth emotions overcame him. He didn't think he would ever say her name again. The cold night air hit him. He shivered, but his face flushed with warmth and passion.

The car's lights disappeared. Quaid stepped inside the warm cottage, locked the door, and sat down in his chair in front of the fireplace.

"Rembrandt, this sure has been some day and tomorrow should be even more interesting."

How could one summer change his life so completely? Two and a half months out of fifty years had controlled his destiny. What ifs, swirled in his head. Why did he leave her behind and not fight for her, why, the one word that had haunted him for years. They had told each other their dreams, made plans for their life together. She was so positive, a free spirit and he played by the rules. If only he had called her. He shouldn't have given up until he heard her voice telling him to move on, but the thought of the words telling him no was too difficult for him to accept. He had been a coward and that had in turn caused him to lose the life he dreamed of. Now he had a chance to relive his past, even if for only one day. The unknown about her was driving him crazy, but he deserved not to know, a punishment of some kind, since he had been a fool to leave her.

The old clock chimed eleven.

The table lamp switched off and Rembrandt followed him into the bedroom.

A Faded Cottage

The bathroom light was bright showing his reflection in the mirror. A man with hair growing out from everywhere, eyebrows, ears, and nose was standing in front of him. His shaky hands touched his beard as frustration grew in his eyes. Staring back at him was a world-renowned artist who couldn't even shave. Nicking his face too many times had put an end to shaving and the thought of facing a barber was too humiliating, a man not able to hold his head still. This was now the real Brenton Quaid Witherspoon, a wild man, a man who would take nothing less but perfection in his life, now a man whose life was far from perfect.

His hands touched his beard. He cringed seeing the grey spotting it. Knowing the wine helped to relax his hands, he picked up the beard trimmer gripping it with both of his hands. The beard trimmer began to glide along his beard, but his hands began to shake uncontrollably. He tightened his grip on the trimmer as frustration built, but it wasn't working. The beard trimmer flew in the air, crashing on the floor in the corner of the bathroom. The beard would stay.

The bathroom light switched off. His shirt pulled over his head hanging it and his jeans on the back of the chair by the window. He laughed pulling his tennis shoes off. "Now tomorrow, Quaid Witherspoon, you do need to wear a pair of socks, ones without holes."

The bed wiggled as he turned the light off. He looked down at Rembrandt. "What are you waiting for, me to go to sleep. Come on, even though you do stink." He laughed. "I guess we're still in that same boat, two scraggly mutts."

The moonlight, shining in around the window curtains lit the room. Quaid's thoughts began, thinking, wondering what tomorrow would be. He chastised himself. He was getting carried away with his dreams, knowing there could be someone else in Sandy's life.

DIANN SHADDOX

A Faded Cottage
A Second Chance

The morning sun was peeking through KC's oldest boy's bedroom window. Sandy pushed the cartoon character bedspread off of her feet and her eyes stared around the poster-filled room. Clanking noises came from the kitchen along with smells floating in the air of coffee and breakfast cooking. Sandy knew KC would be full of questions about last night, scolding her, telling her a woman of her age shouldn't be gallivanting around, spending the evening with a man she hadn't seen in years. KC worried about her and thought the stress of seeing Quaid might be too much for Sandy but they both knew there weren't any words that could stop her now.

One letter had changed her life. What would her life have been like if she had received that letter? Nonetheless, wondering about the letter wasn't going to take the pain of the past away. She at least had her answer to one question. Quaid did care and he had wanted to stay with her, but now she had another question, was there someone else in his life?

The dog-shaped clock said a quarter after seven.

Sandy jumped out of bed excited to meet the day. The room began to spin. She fell onto the bed. *This isn't happening today*, she whispered. *Take a deep breath, Sandy. You're not messing up your one chance.*

The cap snapped on the bottle of medicine and she drank some water letting the pill slide down her throat. She quickly finished her shower, dressing in record time. Nothing was standing in her way. This was going to be their day. Then her dream would be fulfilled.

****

The clock's red eyes glared six o'clock.

Quaid sat up in the white poster bed. He clasped his hands behind his head wiggling his fingers while his mind whirled with questions from last night. Who was Franklin Jackson and were they still married? He tightened his hands with anxiousness growing. Sandy's life was still a mystery to him.

Quaid kicked the covers off his feet, letting his feet slide onto the floor, shivering as he touched the cool wood. The window curtain slid to the side. He felt the coolness of the glass as he stood looking out into the dark morning. The moon was illuminating the darkness like a nightlight in the sapphire sky reflecting on the choppy water and the world seem crispier this morning. He knew he needed to keep moving, that Sandy would be here soon.

Quaid dressed quickly, clean jeans, a fresh t-shirt, adding some cologne, that he never used. He studied the face in the mirror. He was as nervous as he was thirty years ago when he was eighteen that second morning he met Sandy on the beach.

He looked at the clock, time was moving on. He threw dirty clothes, towels, and sheets into a pile next to the washer. He gobbled his bowl of cereal, drank his hot chamomile tea, a routine he did each morning to calm his hands. The coffee pot began to hiss, dripping into the pot as he emptied the dishwasher and then reloaded it. He grabbed the broom on a mission sweeping the kitchen and then the porch. He moved over to the fireplace and he grabbed the bucket, scooping out the cold ashes, adding some new logs placing them perfectly on the grate. Quaid slowly moved around the cottage, checking things out, everything had to be impeccable. He was like a cat in a room full of rockers, so anxious, making his hands shake more.

The coffee that was in the cup in his unsteady hands splashed onto the clean kitchen floor. Today the chamomile tea wasn't working. The refrigerator door swung open showing the bottle of chardonnay. His lips squeezed in disgust reaching for a small plastic glass. The wine would calm his hands at least for a while. Sandy didn't mind the tremors, but he did. The tremors made him feel like an old man, a flaw and he didn't like flaws.

He poured another cup of coffee and sat down in the living room. The clock chimed eight o'clock, thirty minutes to wait.

He wondered if Sandy would show up this morning. Maybe this would be his punishment that she wouldn't show up. He took a sip of the warm coffee blending with the cold wine in his throat. Then his body jerked and his heart stopped beating at the sound of tires crunching in the gravel drive out front.

He lunged out of his chair rushing to the door but slowed his pace, not wanting to seem over anxious.

Sandy's car pulled to a stop and shifted into park in the gravel driveway. She gripped the car's door trying to catch her breath hoping this wasn't a mistake coming back. The front door of the cottage opened and there stood Quaid with the same mischievous grin on his face.

"Good morning, let me help you," Quaid called out, stepping down the porch's steps to the car.

"I guess I'm early," she called out, staring into his blue eyes. Her hand reached over picking up a bag from the deli and another small sack from the front seat. "I hope not too early?"

"No, I have been up for a while," he said relieve she was as anxious as he was.

"There's another bag in the back seat. It's heavier."

"What's this?"

"Dog food. Rembrandt doesn't need to keep eating your food all the time, it's too rich for him," she insisted, smiling at him.

Quaid shrugged his shoulders. "I'm sure he'll appreciate that."

She gave him a quick look. "He's better off eating dog food," she laughed, locking the car door.

Sandy followed Quaid inside and laid the bag of deli food on the kitchen table, setting the other bag in the refrigerator.

"Do you want some coffee or orange juice?" Quaid questioned.

"No thanks, drinking anymore this morning would make me pee and then I'd be in trouble," she said grinning. "You're lucky you can pee anywhere."

That was Sandy, as blunt as ever.

She turned to the laundry room and quickly lifted out a step stool, setting it up next to the tall cabinet in the corner. "Oh, I can't believe it's still here," she said, happily lifting a big basket from the top of the cabinet.

He reached up taking the basket from her. "This isn't the same basket we used to use, is it?"

"It is," she declared, flashing a big smile. She wobbled on the step stool.

"Be careful," he said reaching over catching a hold of her.

Sandy didn't move for a second, feeling the hands from her past around her waist.

"Let's see what's in the basket."

Quaid sat the basket on the kitchen table. He stood next to her smelling her perfume, sweet lilac, the same perfume he'd tried for years to remember. Now the scent was real.

Sandy flipped the tops of the basket open. "Yes, it hasn't been bothered; plates, silverware and even two wine glasses are inside. All we need is the food and wine."

"I can see to the wine. Is there a wine opener in there?"

"Yes, right here," she said swishing the wine opener in the air.

"Wow, that's not the same one we used years ago, is it?"

"It sure is."

She placed all of the food in the basket. "Do you have a jar or a bowl with a lid for Rembrandt's food? We also need some water."

"We're not going away forever," Quaid chuckled, handing her a bowl.

"We need to be prepared," Sandy explained. "You never know what you might need."

It was as if nothing had changed for them. The passion he felt for her was still there.

She turned, moving toward the bedroom. "I have to get something."

Quaid stood in the doorway, arms crossed.

"Stop staring at me, I'm just going to get the old quilt we used to use, if it's still here." The tattered quilt fell into her arms. "No one has touched anything." She didn't move, checking out the room before looking back at him. "You haven't unpacked very much. You sure, you're staying? There are a lot of boxes in here."

"I'm staying, but I never seem to find the time to unpack." His head cocked to the side and his shoulders shrugged. "I never did like to organize things."

"If you need some help unpacking, I don't mind."

"See, you're the one with everything in its place, still as organized as ever. I might have to take you up on the offer."

"Here," she grinned, handing him the frayed quilt. "I need to pee before we leave."

"We have plenty of time. You don't have to rush," he assured caressing the old quilt in his arms.

"Alright," Sandy declared, walking into the kitchen pulling on her ponytail, a nervous habit. She looked at Quaid. "Is something wrong?"

"No," he answered, remembering those days so long ago when she played with her hair. His eyes once more pulled to her left hand, which contained no rings.

She noticed him looking at her hands, but didn't say anything. She picked up the quilt. "You can carry the basket since its heavy."

"Yes it is," he said as he lifted it up in his arms. "I never realized how much you packed."

"You never paid attention to what I brought before, but we had everything we needed."

"I did paid attention, just not to the basket. I was preoccupied with other things on my mind." He hurried past her.

"Uh hum," she called out laughing, letting the door close. Rembrandt ran past them, leaping off the porch.

He wondered what she was thinking and if she was remembering their time so long ago, or maybe he hoped, she was dreaming like him. The lone seagull circled over their heads squawking trying to get their attention. The tall grass rustled in the wind and the wooden boardwalk creaked. Their footprints were left behind as they strolled along the water's edge and waves lapped at their shoes.

Quaid knew Amos was out fishing at his spot down the beach, the opposite way they were going. Amos would be wondering where he and Rembrandt were. But, Levi would soon know the answer and would fill the old man in on the story. The news of Sandy being back would stir up Jana Ann and Karrie. He smiled at that thought.

"This is an exceptional winter day," Sandy finally spoke, hugging the quilt. "The sun is so warm.

"The colors of the day are brilliant," he added, the fervor for painting still burning inside of him.

"Remember the storm?" Sandy said, looking over at him.

The distressed look vanished from his face with just three words.

"Our storm was on a day like today. The morning was so beautiful," she giggled, "you never know what's out to sea."

He slowed his pace. "It was the best day of my life. I'll never forget it." He peered down at her. "The weather was stunning a perfect morning just like today. I remember we didn't pay any attention to the clouds moving in or the wind picking up. I guess we were in a world of our own. We didn't even notice the storm," he chuckled, "until it got so dark and the rain began to hit the roof of the old shack."

"It was also the first of many," she added amused.

It was the first day they made love.

"Do you think your parents knew what we'd done?"

"Now is a little late isn't it to wonder if they knew," he said grinning slowing his walk. "I'm sure they knew something happened. I think our faces told the complete story." Quaid's eyes fell to the ground understanding that was the day he knew he was in love with Sandy, a love that would last a lifetime.

"Your dad started telling you to be more responsible and keep up with the weather. I don't know if he knew we had been to the island, but your mom knew about the island, somehow."

"Mom always seemed to know everything I did. And Levi wouldn't let up, teasing me. I guess my excuse about the boat motor not starting didn't go over very well."

"Not with you grinning so much. You never could lie." She wondered if he still had the same trait.

"You didn't help standing behind me, giggling," he said grinning, trying to reposition the heavy basket on his arm.

"I can't believe we were able to sneak back out to Turtle Island as many times as we did after that."

"The summer sure did go by fast," Quaid admitted.

"Don't start thinking of any regrets, remember?"

"I won't."

"You said you haven't been back to the island. What about all of those vacations over the years with your family? I'm sure your mom and dad came back many times."

89

"They came back every year," he paused, "but the last time I went to the island was with you. I didn't vacation here often after I left that summer. It was too difficult to come back." He took in a deep sigh. "What about you?"

"The last time," Sandy stared out at the water, "was with you. I couldn't ever go back to the island without you, either."

They continued past the marina with its large and small boats bobbling on the water to a small building sitting by itself. The door swung open and Levi's chair flipped back against the wall as he scrambled to get up.

"Sandy, Quaid!" Levi exclaimed, swinging his arms in the air, trying to gain his composure. "This is a sight I didn't think I would ever see again." He stood, hurrying around his large desk. "Boy, it's been years," he cried out, grabbing Sandy.

"We need to rent one of your small boats," Quaid announced as he sat the heavy basket down on the floor. "We're going to Turtle Island."

Levi quietly studied his friend's face, giving Quaid a look, questioning if some memories should stay hidden and was his old friend stirring up more than he could handle. "This must be Rembrandt. Daddy said you had a dog, boy things change fast for you."

Sandy turned to the door. "It was nice to see you again, Levi," she called out, stepping outside with Rembrandt, leaving the friends to talk.

"You sure this is a good idea?" Levi whispered, looking into his old friend's eyes. "You're bringing up a lot of the past along with a lot of pain."

"I've always been one to follow the rules and the only chance I took in my life was on my paintings. Maybe I can fix what I messed up years ago."

"Quaid, sometimes we can't fix the past."

"I have a chance, even if it's just for one day, to relive my past. I can't pass it up. Do you have a boat for us?"

"Alright, I guess I can't blame you. Oh, Jenny…this is going to stir her up." Levi stepped outside, patting his old friend on the back. "She's still as beautiful as ever, isn't, she?"

"Yes," Quaid chuckled, "and it isn't making my life any easier, either."

The old friends kept walking down to the docks to join Sandy and Rembrandt.

"You can take this boat. It has enough gas and the oars, too. Alright you two, if a storm was to come up, remember you need to get back here," Levi called out laughing, looking intently over at his longtime friend. "Don't get caught again in a storm."

"Smart ass!" Quaid snapped back, giving Levi a strong look but holding a huge grin on his face.

Levi helped Sandy into the wobbling boat while Quaid sat the basket between the seats. Rembrandt leaped into the boat next to Sandy and Quaid carefully climbed in the back, holding onto the dock.

The motor accelerated as the small boat bounced along on the waves. The waters were smooth reflecting the sun's rays, and sparkled like small jewels on top of the water. Quaid navigated the boat with many years' experience, leaving the marina behind. Rembrandt's head lay on the side of the boat watching the water splash, sprinkling him.

Sandy was leaning back against the front of the boat, eyes closed. Her hair gently blew in the breeze and her long body lay relaxed, soaking in the warm sun. Quaid's heart raced joining with the hum of the boat motor. The past seem to blend with the present, as if time in between had disappeared completely. This was real. He wasn't dreaming.

Sandy's eyes opened feeling his stare. She took in every feature of Quaid. He might be thirty years older, but he moved as a young man.

DIANN SHADDOX

He was always in top shape, swimming in the ocean, leaping from the waves and water gradually dripping off of his tan body. He was her life. Tears brimmed in her eyes. Was, the word had haunted her for years. She wanted to tell him all of her secrets, but it wasn't the right time, letting them have their one day.

The humming of the boat motor was calming, and his heart slowed to a normal beat. A few larger boats were sailing out to sea not paying any attention to their tiny boat. Gradually the other boats disappeared into the horizon. There, in front of them lay the tiny barrier island, Turtle Island, tucked away from the other barrier islands.

A Faded Cottage
Stepping Back in Time

The boat motor turned off. Silence fell over the morning. A great blue Heron perched on a tree stump in the saltwater marsh and a brown pelican circling over their heads, searching for food, brought Sandy to life.

Quaid lifted the boat motor out of the water. His feet splashed in the cold, shallow water as he slid the small boat upon the sandy beach. Rembrandt leaped from the boat running along the beach leaving them behind.

Sandy and Quaid didn't move as they stood quietly on their island taking everything in around them. So far, things hadn't changed on the small island. Many shrub trees sat bare waiting for spring along with a few old, tall pines standing guard like giants. The one old oak, stunted over the years by the wind, was leaning like an old man with his cane touching the ground, its leaves rustling in the light sea breeze.

"Let's leave everything in the boat and look around," Quaid offered, taking Sandy's hand gently in his, pulling her body close.

They were on their island, safe for the day, neither one worrying about anything. They'd stepped back into their past, something many people never got a chance to do.

Sandy and Quaid quietly walked next to the whispering waves that were parallel to the wild mounds of sand dunes, full of sea oats tussling in the breeze. Sandpipers with short, black legs hurriedly chased their pry running ahead of them. The one large, brown pelican swished down into the blue water with precise accuracy flying away with his catch of the day.

"Quaid," Sandy asked, apprehension in her voice, "tell me what you did after you left here?" She looked away from his staring eyes out toward the ocean. "Did you marry the girl you talked about at the beginning of the summer?"

"Yes," he admitted, squeezing his mouth tight, shaking his head. The words were difficult to say. "I went back to New York and a few years later I married Karen. We never had children."

"Oh, I see," Sandy got quiet.

"We weren't married long. It seemed Karen had her own dreams. We divorced after five years. It was a big mistake on my part. My paintings became my life, my family for all those years." His voice became soft, "I never married again."

"Did you finally take over the family business? Your father sure was pushing you to."

"No, Bradley took over the business with his son, Chandler. My life was my paintings until a few years ago." His head ducked looking at his hands as he rubbed them together.

She stopped walking and spun around facing him looking up into those blue eyes. "I heard about your hands from Jenny. She didn't tell me much about your life except a little about your tremors and that Amos and Levi were helping you."

"It hasn't been easy," he said angrily, gripping his hands together tightly. "The last few years have been difficult. The stares are so tough. I understand most people don't mean to be cruel but even my close friends can't comprehend it. How could a man with hand's able to paint great works of art suddenly lose control?"

"That had to be hard on you."

"I couldn't take the stares. I guess I needed to wear a sign--I'm not nervous, I can't control my Goddamn hands." He held his hands out in front of him. "They've let me down and won't do as I want. I thought I was going crazy; maybe I did for a while and depression sat in. I had to leave New York and find a new life. I had to live away from the stares, away from my friends."

"I was sorry to hear you'd quit painting," she spoke in a gentle voice as her fingers stroked his arm.

"The critics put an end to my painting; they destroyed my art with their critiques."

"When did the tremors start?"

"It was about ten years ago my hands began to shake more and more. I thought it was arthritis. I went to doctor after doctor and they dismissed it. Then we thought it was the onset of Parkinson's but I soon learned I had Essential Tremors, or ET, a rhythmic trembling of your hands and body."

"Can't they do something about it? There has to be medicine..."

He tightened his fisted hands. "I took medicine for a while, but it made me drowsy and it made me feel strange then it finally stopped working and."

"You can't give up," she interrupted. "You have to fight."

"I don't know. I guess I've been feeling sorry for myself, especially this last year, my life hasn't been worth living." he swallowed. "Trying to do tedious strokes with my paintbrush has been too much for me. People have been cruel. Being out in public is so difficult. I've been hiding away for the last few months, only being around Amos and Levi."

"Has it helped?" She questioned, holding onto Quaid's arm, looking caringly at him. "Being away from people?"

"The truth?"

"The truth is all you can tell, isn't it?"

"It hasn't helped. I still get mad at myself when I try to do things. Simple things have become complicated. Things we all take for granted, writing, signing my name. I have trouble dressing, buttoning my shirt, even trying to trim my beard," he laughed, rubbing his face.

"I like you in a beard," she said kindly. "It makes you look distinguished, but you could have your beard trimmed by a barber."

He kicked the sand. "No, my head trembles and I can't take the stares. I guess I have too much pride. It's as if my body is in overload. I'm also very sensitive to cold. I don't pay any attention to my hands shaking unless I'm trying to do something that takes a steady hand. It's not like I was a surgeon or anything important but my paintings were my life."

She reached out taking his hands. "You're still the same man and nothing has changed. Don't let this ruin your life." She held his hands in her hand and he let his hands quiver, as she massaged his hands. "Don't try so hard."

Her hand reached up caressing his face pulling his face to her. She tiptoed letting her lips touch his.

He wrapped his arms around her just as he did that first night they were together and they kissed for the first time in thirty years.

Tears built in his eyes. His hand tremors had brought him back to Hathaway Cove. He knew he never would have come back to the beach if he had been able to continue to paint.

Her hands dropped to her sides as they broke apart. "Let's go see…" she said earnestly, turning running up the old path, not finishing her sentence.

He ran after her and in no time, they both slid to a stop. In front of them was the weathered grey fishing shack standing worn, leaning some, but in fair shape.

"People are still coming out here," he declared, looking around the building. "There are some fish bones by the cleaning table that aren't very old."

He stepped passed. "There might be some wild animals living in here. We need to be careful," he said.

Slowly the doorknob turned and the door swung open squeaking with an uncanny sound telling its age. In front of them, except for cobwebs hanging all around, was the same room with the leaning reddish rocked fireplace, just as it looked thirty years ago.

Sand was all over the floor and one of the two windows was cracked, but still standing, letting sunlight glimmer through, making kaleidoscope shadows.

The old table and chairs sat in the corner of the small room, one of the chair legs missing, leaning against the wall, trying to stay stable. A small, brown lizard ran past them over to the fireplace.

"Oh," Sandy called out, "a big, vicious animal..."

Quaid turned around, his face twisted in a frown.

She laughed. "We'll have to name him. You liked pirates years ago. I remember some of the stories you used to tell me when we'd sit out on the beach late at night. Your stories were so realistic, making me believe and dream about pirates coming to shore. So," her head swung back as if she was making an important proclamation, "I think we should name him Captain Claws. He does have fierce looking feet."

"Alright, I get the point, but he's not the animal I was worried about. Captain Claws can stay," Quaid chuckled, shaking his head.

Sandy stood in the doorway looking at Quaid. Sunlight shown on his older face, but still the same boy she had fallen in love with right here that wonderful hot summer day, the place where they first made love.

The room spun and her hand reached out gripping the wall, steadying herself. Her heart beat like a man that was dancing on hot coals. Her eyes pulled to Quaid, he hadn't notice her clutching the wall. She gripped the wall tight letting her fingernails dig in. This was their day and nothing was going to interfere.

"The old place is worn, a little like me, I guess" Quaid added, wiping the mantel with his fingers. "I can't believe this place is still in this good of shape. I never knew how well it was constructed. I guess it was another reason we didn't hear the storm." He moved over by the windows looking outside, "we were…busy."

"Quaid, look!" Sandy cried out.

He spun around trying to catch his breath, quickly understanding her excitement.

"I can't believe our names are still here," she whispered, looking down at the bottom of the wall.

He squatted down on the floor next to the wall and his trembling hand reached out and touched the grey planks. "Sandy and Quaid forever," he whispered, seeing the words in their dark, red paint, still legible in the meticulousness writing of an artist's hand, just as he'd left them thirty years ago.

"I guess some things are meant to be," she declared. Sandy knelt down on the floor next to him staring at the words.

His arm reached over, pulling her near, understanding what she was thinking, feeling her breathing next to him, the same sensations gushed through his body the same as he felt thirty years ago. Time had stopped for them and he didn't want it to begin. He believed they could stay here away from everyone and everything, but a noise startled him. His head swung to the door.

"Rembrandt, he's been running all over the island," she added, petting the dog.

"Not merely running, peeing all over the island, marking his territory. This is his island now," Quaid teased.

"Don't pay any attention to him, Rembrandt. Yes, this is your island too."

"Let's go back to the boat and get the food," Quaid offered. "Where do you want to have our picnic?"

"Let's go to the other cove that was always full of wildflowers. Maybe some will be blooming." She grinned, looking up at Quaid.

"We do seem to lose track of time when we're in this fishing shack. Sandy moved over by the fireplace and her finger touched the old rocks. "Goodbye, Captain Claws. You need to see to this place for me until I come back."

Quaid smiled watching her having a conversation with a lizard, but worry was taking over. He noticed her clutching the mantel trying to steady herself and as the redness from the sun on her skin faded, Quaid couldn't help but see her face was becoming pallid and drawn.

Sandy saw the apprehension in his face and she grabbed his arm, bringing him back from his thoughts. "This place will be great after we get rid of the cobwebs and some of the sand," she declared, stepping down the old rickety steps, holding onto Quaid. "I love it here," she squealed. Her ponytail flew into the air as she spun around in a circle. Her hands reached out grabbing Quaid's arm, pulling him near. "This is real, right? I'm not dreaming or anything, am I?"

"Yes, it's real, our dream." Relief came over him knowing she was ready to come back to the island. "We can clean this old place up. We'll bring some things with us next time. It'll be fun."

His arm wrapped around her as they walked along the beach, letting Rembrandt run ahead. The sun now high in the sky shown down warming the day as the scent of warm sand and pine needles floated on the cool sea breeze. Quaid lifted the basket from the boat and Sandy pulled out the old quilt.

"C'mon, over there," she pointed. She took off weaving through the palmetto bushes hugging the quilt.

"Be careful around those bushes, there could be snakes!" Quaid yelled, trying to catch up. But Rembrandt was right by Sandy's side, watching out for her.

"This is it," she cried out, trying to lay the blanket down on the sand, getting frustrated with the wind blowing the quilt.

"Here, let me help." Quaid leaned over, sitting the basket down on the edge of the blanket, stopping the blanket from blowing in the wind. He squatted down on his knees by the basket, his eyes on Sandy.

Sandy slid in next to him, lifting the bottle of wine from the basket. "You open this while I get Rembrandt some food and water."

"I see where I rate," he exclaimed, leaning back on the blanket watching her prepare Rembrandt's food.

She leaned over close, cupping his face in her hands. "You'll always be first for me," she said softly, stroking his face.

She placed Rembrandt's bowl of food on a towel, pouring him some fresh water. The dog began to drink, slurping the water, letting it drip from his face.

"There," Quaid said with delight as the cork popped from the bottle. "Hold the wine glasses."

"Good job," she said carefully, handing his glass to him. "Here's to old times." Her wine glass swayed in the air gently touching his wineglass to her. "May they continue forever."

The wine tingled trickling down his throat, understanding the wine wasn't going to make sitting here on the quilt next to her any easier.

Sandy scooted near him, slipping her wineglass into the special spot on the basket's side. She lifted out the deli sandwiches and potato salad, fixing both their plates. "I thought sandwiches would do nicely."

"The sandwiches are great," he mumbled, swallowing a big bite. "You know we couldn't have a better view in any restaurant anywhere."

Sandy and Quaid sat in silence eating their sandwiches, sipping their wine with the seagulls squawking overhead, waiting for bites of food.

He leaned back on his arms watching the waves playing their game with Rembrandt. The day was perfect as the tall pines swished moaning in the breeze.

Remember the night," Sandy whispered, "the week before you left when we stayed out here on the island until very late? The stars were so bright in the black sky we believed we could touch them."

"I remember.

"It was magical, so quiet with only the waves lapping at the beach.

"It was wonderful," he sighed, "it was the night of the shooting star. I've never seen a star so brilliant in color, so huge and staying so long, gliding across the sky."

She leaned near him, gazing into his eyes. "I won't ever forget how the star swished across the sky leaving a path of sparkles. It was if it was shining especially for us."

"And we both made our wish," he whispered, turning his head from her, getting quiet.

"My wish is coming true, maybe a few years late," she said, gently touching his hand.

He took in a deep breath. Why did he leave her?

"Listen to those waves. They each have a story to tell," she said softly, letting go of his hand, lying back on the quilt and closing her eyes.

Quaid couldn't help but notice Sandy was becoming paler and clearly, Sandy wasn't ready to talk about herself.

"You haven't eaten much, are you alright?" he asked worriedly.

"I'm fine, a little tired," she assured. "It's so relaxing here it always makes me want to sleep, remember?"

"Yes, I remember," he said quietly, leaning back on the quilt next to her, forcing himself not to ask any more questions.

Sandy scooted over by him, laying her head on his chest closing her eyes.

His arm wrapped around her warm body as she gently took in soft breaths and drifted off to sleep. He'd get his answers from her another time. All he needed now was just to hold her in his arms. She needed rest and this was the perfect spot with the sun's rays beaming down warming the island this twentieth day of December.

Quaid lay quietly looking up at the fluffy, white clouds floating across the sky making shapes of cartoon caricatures. Clouds were one of the first things he drew when he was young, catching the characters before they disappeared into the sky. He listened to the waves lapping at the shore. The grass wrestled in the breeze and he could see Rembrandt with his head down resting, tired from his antics with the waves. Harmony had fallen over the world.

His eyes took in the colors of the sky, blending with the swirling clouds floating by, remembering how it felt to bring a painting to life. Tears welled as he held Sandy while she slept so peacefully. She was real and he was living his dream if only for a day, not worried about having all the answers or about his life.

Sandy woke full of energy.

"This day has been so wonderful," she paused, "being back here." She wiggled, stretching her arms. "I didn't realize how much I missed being at the beach and our island."

Quaid's mind spun, wanting to tell her she could stay forever. "I'm glad you got some rest." His face moved close to her face and their lips met.

The palms of her hands gently pushed against his chest as she sat up looking out to sea.

Quaid grinned back at her with his mischievous little laugh.

"The sea's calm, no storm today," she said teasingly. "My little nap was better than a full night's sleep." Her fingers caressed his arm. "I know it doesn't matter but what time is it?"

"A little after three," he answered, looking at his watch, "it's getting a little cooler with the sun not directly on us."

"We should go back and stop by the marina for the shrimp. We can come back here another day," she assured him.

"Shrimp sounds great," he answered.

She shook the quilt letting grains of sand fly into the wind.

He watched always mesmerized by the sand. He had tried to capture the sand on canvas, its mystery, but he hadn't been able to, another one of his regrets.

"Listen to all the birds, they're singing so beautiful," Sandy said, settling into the boat.

"Birds are always happy at the beginning and end of the day, but they seem even more excited than normal. Maybe they're glad we're leaving," he replied.

"No, I think their saying goodbye and come back," she explained, smiling at him.

Quaid did a big shove, jumping into the boat making it bobble in the shallow water as the motor fell into the clear water. Quaid steered the small craft out into the deep water. The air was cooling and the waves had tiny white caps making the boat weave along, skipping over the water, heading around the side of the small island.

"It's funny how close the island is to the marina," he said, "but it seems so far away when we're there."

"It does have its own mystic. Oh," she moaned, "I hope no one bothers it."

"Me either," he agreed, squinting his eyes as he thought about the island while guiding the small boat near the dock.

The boat motor shut off.

Sandy climbed out of the boat with a rope in her hand, tying the boat to the pier just as she did thirty years ago. Rembrandt leaped from the boat and stood on the dock beside her, waiting patiently.

Quaid studied Sandy and Rembrandt as he finished tying his ropes. Rembrandt didn't move until Sandy began to walk as she weaved from side to side, the old dock creaking under their feet.

Quaid could see the marina on the small hill not far from Levi's small building. "I'll go get some shrimp. Do you need anything else for tonight?"

"You said you had some rice, right?"

"Yes."

"I brought some vegetables, so we should be fine."

"How much shrimp?"

"Get about two pounds," she replied, her arms crossed hugging her shivering body in the cool breeze.

"No problem," he assured. "Here." He sat the basket down by her feet. "I'll be right back." He hurriedly stepped up the long wooden steps and rushed inside the marina.

"Hey, Quaid, how're things going?" Bobby asked in his worn overalls, his oversize grin showing his yellow-toothed smile the result of years of dipping tobacco. "Or do I have to ask?" The short, round man exclaimed, hurrying over to the large window peering down on the beach.

"Levi...right?" Quaid questioned. Small towns. Gossip was considered a pastime around here. He moved over to the display case staring at the fish and shrimp.

"Naw," Bobby chuckled, "why would you ever think Levi would gossip?" The man sniggered, showing his freckles. He narrowed his beady eyes. "You should know news travels fast around here. What can I do for you?"

"I need some shrimp."

"Sounds like a good meal tonight. Things must be going well...huh, cooking dinner for her."

"Okay Bobby, just get me some shrimp, about two pounds."

"You're no fun, Quaid," Bobby chuckled again, taking one more look down at the beach, hurriedly filling a bag with shrimp. "They're on the house. You sure have stirred up this place. You have a good evening."

"Thanks, Bobby," Quaid called back to his old friend, pushing the Marina door open.

Quaid carefully descended the old wooden steps making his way down to the beach, but his eyes stayed glued on Sandy as she stood looking out to the water her back to him. Quaid slowed his pace.

Rembrandt wiggled and Sandy turned around watching Quaid, a smile on her face. He used to think he was dreaming watching her walk down the beach swinging her sandals in her hands, her long hair flowing behind her, her soft summer dress blowing in the breeze.

He took the basket from her placing the shrimp inside.

"What went on up there?"

"How do you know these things?" He questioned.

"Your face. It's an open book. Always has been," she declared as a little smile came over her face.

"Levi is talking too much. It seems everyone knows you're back in town and our story is going around."

"Good, this old place needs something to happen." Her hands reached up bringing his face near, kissing him. "Maybe a kiss will stir them up," she said laughing, looking up at the marina windows.

He laughed. "It sure stirred me up," he replied with a wink.

Rembrandt ran ahead of them playing with the waves. They silently walked along the shoreline, as they listened to the evenings sounds watching the sun begin to set.

"The air is getting cooler. You were right. The temperature seems to drop fast when the sun goes down," she added, shuddering following Quaid into the kitchen.

Quaid sat the basket on the kitchen table and pulled out the fresh shrimp.

Alright," Sandy said excitedly, washing her hands. "I need to start cooking."

"What can I do to help?"

"You can cut some vegetables while I peel and devein the shrimp. And you do need to start the rice. We need to sauté the vegetables in olive oil then I want to sauté the shrimp after I let the vegetables simmer for a while."

Quaid lifted the knife, but just stood there.

Sandy stopped working. "I'm sorry Quaid, I wasn't thinking."

"I will cut the vegetables," he said still gripping the knife.

"You don't have to cut the vegetable very small. It's fine, if you don't want to do this," she assured him, seeing the frustration on his face.

He didn't speak. The artist who couldn't even hold a knife to cut vegetables. His trembling hands began to drop hunks of vegetables in the sizzling skillet, letting their aroma fill the cottage.

****

Sandy's hands were busy working on the shrimp but she could feel his stare as he moved around the kitchen. Warmness came over her body, an excitement she hadn't felt in years, when Quaid began to hum. Soft words flowed as he started singing their song in his perfect pitch. Sandy closed her eyes remembering sitting on the beach late at night listening to their music play, Quaid singing along with the song.

She laid the clean shrimp on the platter taking in a deep breath, slowly turning around trying to collect her thoughts.

"Anything else?" He questioned, still humming the song.

"The shrimp doesn't take long so I'll cook it in a few minutes. How about a glass of wine while the vegetables simmer?"

"You want cabernet or chardonnay?" He asked, going to the pantry.

"The red wine we had last night was great."

"Alright," Quaid said, pouring the wine into two glasses. How silly his life had become, the simple act of pouring wine without splashing was now a great accomplishment. He handed Sandy her wineglass trying not to let it splash. "I can't wait to eat. It smells wonderful in here."

Sandy took a small sip of wine moving into the living room. "I do love to smell fresh vegetables cooking."

His wineglass steadily cupped in his hands, he followed Sandy into the living room.

"We need a fire," he said, squatting down by the hearth. Rembrandt yawned, his eyes staring back at Quaid, exhausted from the day's antics.

Sandy settled into her chair. The lighter clicked. Quaid stood from the floor straightening his body watching the flames dance popping in the quiet night.

Sandy slowly sipped her wine, not worrying about anything tonight, her health or her emotions. This was their night and she wasn't going to control herself. She'd always been in control of her life, a trait she learned from her mother. Tonight, this one night, she wasn't going to think about anything but being right here in the old cottage with Quaid. She slid out of her chair onto the floor in front of the fire, taking in the warmth.

"Who is Jana Ann?"

Quaid slid from his chair onto the floor next to Sandy, moving his fingers around on his chin. "How do you know about Jana Ann?"

"You called her name out yesterday when I showed up."

"Right."

"So who is she?"

"Maybe I'll keep who she is a secret."

"Quaid!"

"Alright," he said laughing, "she's the realtor who helped me find this house and she's been bringing me food." He shrugged his shoulders. "I think she feels sorry for me."

Sandy turned her head. Her eyes glared. "Yea, right. Are you really that naïve?"

He grinned.

"So the dishes are hers and she brought you cookies, too?"

"The dishes are hers, but Karri brought me the cookies."

"Karri, oh…" Sandy got quiet.

"Sandy, it's no big deal. They feel sorry for me. I guess they don't think I can take care of myself. They're only being kind."

"Uh um," she said, her eyes narrowing as she slowly sipped her wine watching the fire, unable to look at him. She took in a deep breath. "You know, I went to New York one time about ten years after you left here with one of my friends."

Quaid moaned.

"Don't wonder so much," she laughed, finally turning her eyes toward him. "It was a girlfriend who went with me. We went to see a couple of musicals on Broadway. New York is so busy."

"I loved living there when I was working on my paintings and doing art shows," he said, gripping his wine glass tightly. "But now it's time to slow down and live a different kind of life."

"You seem to miss New York."

"No, not New York. Painting." He heaved a sigh and his eyes turned from her face toward the flames.

Sandy shook her head seeing hurt on his face. Her hand reached over touching his. "You know," she began timidly, "I went to one of your art premiers when I was there..." She became quiet, taking in a deep breath.

"You were at one of my art premiers?" he exclaimed, turning back to her.

"Yes, your pieces were marvelous, so beautiful. I knew you'd be famous." She got quiet, biting her lip, remembering.

He didn't say anything as he sat in silence staring at her, waiting for her to finish her story.

"You were signing your paintings and some autographs while I was there. My friend got one."

"Why didn't you try and talk to me?"

"I couldn't. I didn't want to disrupt you so I stood by the door. You looked over my way. It was strange, maybe you sensed me staring. I had to jump back behind some people so you wouldn't see me. You sat there and shook your head, but you glanced my way again a bit later."

"I wish you'd come up to me." Quaid paused. "Maybe things could have been different," he pulled in a deep sigh. "But I guess not if you thought I left you on purpose." His head weaved back and forth and his mouth tightened.

"Well, it's water under the bridge and we can't do a damn thing about it. But we have now," she declared, swishing her hair from her face.

"You're right, but I sure wish you'd spoken to me. Sandy, why did you leave so many of your personal things in the house when you sold it? Quilts, dishes, the basket..." He looked into her green eyes. "The painting?"

"I was going through a rough time back then," she said, fiddling nervously with her hair. "I was getting a divorce. All of these things were a reminder of what my life could have been. It was a difficult time. I'd lost you and then Franklin."

"Franklin Jackson?"

"Yes, but how did you know?"

"Jana Ann told me the cottage was sold by Franklin Jackson to Maggie Hendry."

"Yes, Maggie is a good friend of mine. She wanted me to keep the cottage, but like I said, it had too many memories," she gulped for air, looking up at the painting. "I felt like a failure."

"How long were you married?" He asked even though he told himself to let it go.

"Eight years. Franklin's an architect and a good man, but we didn't have the same dreams. He got tired of me being unrealistic, impracticable and too carefree. I learned soon after we were married that he was responsible enough for both of us."

"I understand." Quaid could see it was all she was going to say on the subject. "I'm glad you're not practical."

She did a slight smile. Her mind wondered thinking about the difference in Quaid and Jackson. Quaid, a dreamer seeing the beauty in the world, and Jackson a man of facts believing dreams were a waste of time.

The fire popped. She looked over at Quaid, as he sat quietly watching her.

"Being back here is wonderful. I only hope I have enough time…" her words faded away as the buzzer beeped in the kitchen. "I better go check the vegetables and put the shrimp on to sauté."

"The rice should be done by now," he answered. Worriedly, he stood wringing his hands together. Sandy knew he sensed something was wrong. He was right. She was hiding another secret. He wasn't going to push for an answer, not yet.

"How's the shrimp?"

"It's ready." She opened the cabinet door pulling out a large bowl and two plates, setting the plates on the table along with the silverware. "Sit down. I'll finish up."

"Wow," he moaned, taking a bite of food. "This is delicious; you do know how to cook."

"Only a few things. Don't forget I'm making some chowder next time I come. I have to get back home tomorrow, but I'll try and come back this weekend if it's alright," she said, taking a breath, hoping she wasn't being too aggressive. "Oh," she added nervously, leaning back in her chair, "next weekend is Christmas." She looked up from the table, shaking her head. "I don't want to interfere with your Christmas plans. I'll try for another weekend."

"What plans? Next weekend would be great. The holidays are just going to be me and Rembrandt," he hesitated. "I don't know if I can pull off cooking Christmas dinner."

"Don't worry, I'll prepare my chowder and bring Christmas dinner," Sandy reassured. "You don't have to cook anything."

"Sounds good to me," he admitted. He sat studying every inch of her, the smile flowing from ear to ear, the curve of her face and the softness of her lips. His body jerked realizing how much he was staring.

"You will have to let me know what I need to buy at the grocery. Do you like eggnog?"

"Yes," she grinned. "Do you have some bourbon?"

"I sure do."

"Good," she said. "I'll make a list of what you can get at the grocery for me." She paused, "I forgot you don't get out around people. Levi gets your groceries. I hope he won't mind."

"I'll see to getting what we need don't worry."

Sandy stood, picking up the plates and going toward the sink. The dishes slid into the dishwasher. The sprayer swished the water around rinsing the sink, but her thoughts continued. She wondered how close he had come to the women and if one was special.

"You'll have some leftovers."

"Extra food always helps."

"Jana Ann and Karrie might be stopping by with some food, too," she added, jealousy showing in her voice as her body tensed.

Quaid moved over to her, reaching his arms around her, staring at their reflection in the dark window over the sink. "You never have to worry about someone else. You never did," he whispered in her ear before kissing her soft lips.

She kissed him back, teasing him with so much passion. Her arms wrapped around his neck and she played with his long hair, their bodies tight together.

Neither said a word as he led her into the bedroom. Their eyes stayed fixed on each other as they lay down on the old bed, the present blending with the past in the light of the full moon shining in through the huge window.

Her hand reached up stroking his face, touching his beard. She snuggled next to him as passion took over her mind and body. The warm emotions of the past were emerging and she couldn't deny her love. She closed her eyes, remembering the touch of his hand gliding down her body with so much ease, knowing the difference in the past and present. She remembered the first time lying on the old quilt in the fishing shack, Quaid holding her tight.

Quaid's body throbbed with fervor. He could feel her curvy body. He remembered the touch of her skin, the feel of her ample shape. Their love was spontaneous then just as it was now, a perfect love, as he felt her body under his, as their bodies became one. He didn't want to unwrap his arms from around her, afraid she would disappear.

She reached up caressing his face and she whispered, "I love you, Quaid Witherspoon."

"I've always loved you, Sandy Jamison, or whatever your name is," Quaid replied.

"I'm Sandy Jamison and I haven't remarried," she whispered playing with his long hair.

"Are you going back to KC's tonight?"

"I'd like to stay here tonight if it's alright?"

"You can stay here forever."

Rembrandt did a soft bark, making them both laugh.

"I don't know if he's agreeing with me about you staying or if he needs to go outside, maybe both." Quaid climbed out of bed, slipping his jeans on as Sandy followed with a quilt wrapped around her body.

They went to the door and Rembrandt ran out into the starry night. They stood on the porch, listening to the waves.

Sandy cuddled close to him. "This is nice. We're both home at least for a while," she said.

"Yes we are and it's pleasant out tonight," he added, hearing the breeze rustling the old squatted oak on the side of the cottage.

"The stars seem even brighter than normal," she said in a soft voice.

"I can't wait until it warms up and we can sit on the porch. I love watching the moon flickering out on the water, making you wonder what could be way out in the ocean."

Rembrandt ran past them into the living room.

"Maybe some of your pirates are out there," she added, not moving from the door. "I love listening to the frog's ribbiting joining the chirping of the summer cricket on warm summer nights."

"Do you remember when we took walks on the beach at night with the moon shining down and we would chase those tiny crabs?" he asked.

"Yes, it was like the moon pulled the tiny crabs out of their homes each night. They were so cute running around. I bet Rembrandt loves chasing them."

"I'm sure he will.

I can't wait to watch him but I hope I'll be..." her voice trailed off. She turned around not finishing her sentence, wiping her eyes, not knowing what the future held for them. "I need to get my things from the car," she said anxiously. She picked up her car keys laying by the dishes, a reminder of the other women in his life. She stepped out into the crisp night air tugging the quilt tight around her body as she unlocked the car.

Quaid picked up her brown suitcase and small bag placing them on a bench by the end of the bed.

Sandy pulled out her pink pj shirt and butterfly bottoms, and went into the bathroom taking her other small bag with her.

She slipped on the pj's then she opened several bottles of medicine. She stared into the mirror at her drained face seeing tears well in her eyes. *No tears of sadness. Only tears of love.*

She combed her long hair, dampening a cloth, dabbing her face, trying to get some color back in her cheeks. She closed the bottles putting them back into the bag before hurrying to the living room.

She snuggled in the chair next to Quaid listening to soft music not thinking or worrying about the future.

DIANN SHADDOX

DIANN SHADDOX

A Faded Cottage

Christmas Spirit

The next morning the sun filtered through the edges of the curtains making shadows on the bed. Quaid looked over and sighed, Sandy was actually lying there beside him, sleeping sweetly. He didn't move for a while watching her sleep but finally lifted the quilts, letting his feet fall to the floor.

Rembrandt's head popped up and the dog did one leap and was down on the floor, careful not to shake the bed.

Quaid's jeans and shirt slipped on and noiselessly he closed the bedroom door. "I'm worried about her," Quaid said to Rembrandt.

He pushed the button on the coffee pot and opened the back door as Rembrandt ran past.

"Alright, it's going to be a great day," he said softly into the cool morning, letting his feet wiggle on the cold porch planks. He closed the back door trying to be quiet, not wanting to make any noise to wake Sandy.

The coffee rumbled as it finished dripping into the pot. He poured himself a cup, careful not to over fill it, a lesson he'd learned early on with ET. He sat down in his chair thinking over the past few days.

Mornings were so peaceful in the cottage. The sun would shine through all the kitchen windows, shimmering on everything, making the day feel so fresh and clean. He slowly sipped his coffee pondering his life, how it had changed so dramatically in the past year, and now so much more in the past two days.

"Good morning," a sweet voice came from the bedroom, bringing his thoughts back to the present. "Coffee, great."

"It's decaf."

"Decaf is perfect. Did you sleep well?" She asked, sitting down next to him in her chair, pulling her knees up beneath her.

"Best night ever. How about you?" He paused, "You've been tired."

"I slept like a baby," she answered, bringing her coffee cup to her lips. "It's too bad I have to leave this morning. I can see this is going to be a beautiful day. I'd love to take another walk on the beach."

"You can stay if you want."

"I have appointments I can't change, but I'll be back soon," she assured, cupping her warm mug in her hands.

"Do you want breakfast," he offered. "I've learned to cook eggs and toast." Quaid sat up in his chair, rubbing his hands together feeling the tremors.

"No thanks," she smiled at him. "I think I might eat some cereal. I'm not very hungry."

"I do have a few boxes of cereal, you can choose one."

"I need a shower first," she laughed, combing her hair with her fingers. "I'd better get ready." She quickly sat her cup in the sink. "If I don't watch the time, I'll sit here all morning."

"I'd love for you to stay," he declared, pulling her to him.

"I'll be back soon," she added, letting her fingers run through his thick hair.

Quaid began to clean out the dishwasher, but she was done with her shower before he finished. "Boy, you're fast," he said, turning around. "You need to eat some cereal before you get on the road."

"Yes, sir," she chuckled, sitting down at the table.

He sat down in a chair across from her at the table, pouring cereal into an old green bowl. He kept staring, not able to take his eyes from her.

"What is it?" she questioned, "Is my hair still messed up?"

"No, you're wonderful. This is what life is about. Waking up with someone you love."

"I agree," she answered putting her cereal bowl in the sink. She squatted down on the floor. "Rembrandt, you take care of Quaid for me and I'll be back in a few days," she assured, rubbing his fur, his dark eyes staring back. She stood up and her hand touched Quaid's arm. "You take care. I love you."

The words hit him hard, taking his breath away, leaving him struggling to keep his composure. He reached his arms around her, pulling her tight. "I love you, too. It's so difficult to let you go," he whispered, kissing her. "Are we both dreaming?"

"If it's a dream, I never want to wake up," she said. "Quaid, don't look so worried. It's only going to be a few days," she promised. Sandy undid his arms, going into the bedroom. When she returned, she was carrying her suitcase.

"Here," he said, hurrying to help.

Sandy didn't move, pulling in a deep breath. "I left some of my things in the bedroom and bath. I hope that's alright?" She hesitated. "I wouldn't want to disrupt Jana Ann and Karrie."

"Sandy, they haven't and won't ever be in my bedroom," he replied.

"Quaid," she said, stepping down the porch steps. "Stop worrying, I'll see you Christmas Eve."

He lifted the suitcase into the back seat, kissed her one last tine, and slowly moved back to the porch with Rembrandt watching her drive away.

"Well boy, it's the two of us for a few days. The first thing on my list is a Christmas tree. Guess I had better get some lights and ornaments along with it. Then I have to get Sandy a present, maybe several," he added, getting himself wound up.

He went into the bedroom to clean, but the bed was made and everything was in its place. In the bathroom on the counter were some of her hair things. "This is for real," he whispered.

Quaid stood wondering how his life could have turned around so fast, but something in the back of his mind kept nagging at him. *Don't make problems where there aren't any.*

"Alright, Rembrandt, do you want to go with me to the hardware?" he asked, looking down at the dog. He clinched his hands together. "You know, I'll be around people, but I don't have any other choice," he said, ringing his hands. "I made a promise, I'd see to everything."

Rembrandt jumped into the truck. The key turned and the engine of the old truck hummed. Quaid had bought the nine-year-old truck from Amos paying more than he should, so Amos could buy the red truck he had been wanting.

The rocks crunched under the tires driving down Gull Lane. The truck stopped at the next intersection turning left onto Hudson Street. The old hardware, sitting at the end of the street, looked the same as it did a hundred years ago with its old clapboards greyed and its two huge doors opened wide. The truck bounced to a stop as Quaid parked near the front doors.

"No, boy," Quaid said putting his hand up, "you stay put. I'll be right back."

Quaid stepped inside the old hardware store.

A young girl about fifteen stood near the counter busily stacking some boxes. "Good morning, sir," she said kindly with a big smile making dimples in her cheeks. "Can I help you with something?"

"I need to get a Christmas tree," Quaid announced, "along with some lights and ornaments."

"Alright," the young girl responded as she hurriedly moved from behind the counter. She began gathering boxes of lights, laying them back on the counter. "Our ornaments are down that aisle," she said pointing. "You need to pick through them and choose what you like, unless you want help?" she questioned.

"I could use some help," Quaid added as he stared at all the different ornaments. "If you don't mind."

"I don't mind, this is fun. You have to have an angel or star for the top of the tree to make it perfect and a tree skirt will make the tree look great."

"Oh, the star has so many beautiful colors, I'll take it. Pick a tree skirt for me and I'll walk out front and choose a tree."

"Mister, you'll also need a tree stand if you don't have one," the young girl called out.

"Do I need anything else?"

"Maybe an extension cord," came a familiar voice from an older man standing next to the door. "Quaid Witherspoon, how you been doing?"

"Tommy...it's been a long time, you're looking good," Quaid called out, looking into the old face of the young boy from his youth. "You own this hardware?"

Tommy patted him on the back. "Yep, my grandfather left it to me. My dad didn't want to run it so here I am. I heard you were around stirring everyone up, living in Miss Eula's old cottage on Gull Lane. Sandy's back, right?"

"Yes, she left for a few days, but she's coming back Christmas Eve so I want everything perfect for Christmas." Quaid's lips tightened and his eyes peered down at his hands. "I guess I'm doing pretty well."

"Well, I really can't complain. You know my granddaddy worked here until he was ninety-two, so we have a long way to go. Judy will take good care of you, she's my youngest daughter."

Quaid smiled at the young girl seeing she looked just like her mother Mary Ann did thirty years ago, with the same long, dark blonde hair and blue-green eyes. "Judy sure has been a lot of help. There's a lot more to putting up a Christmas tree than I thought."

"You're the famous artist from New York," Judy exclaimed. "Wow, I heard about you."

"Thanks for helping me."

"No problem, I'll get everything ready for you. Your tree will be gorgeous," Judy said, her face beaming with pride.

"Quaid, this is a good tree, it's fat with a lot of branches. It will be beautiful," Tommy said confidently, weaving some rope around a small spruce. "Let's get it into your truck."

Quaid opened the tailgate of the truck and Tommy helped him lift the fat tree into the back.

"Nice looking dog," Tommy offered, pushing the tailgate of the truck closed.

"He's a great dog." Quaid turned back to the store. "Now I need to see what all Judy has done."

"I think she's thought of everything," Tommy said, smiling. "You have a Merry Christmas, Quaid. Tell Sandy I said hi. It's kind of nice having everyone back around again, like the summer we all hung out together, it almost makes me feel young again."

"We did have fun back then. Maybe we should get together?" Quaid questioned, surprising himself that he wanted to be around people.

"Sounds good to me. I know Mary Ann would love the idea."

"You tell Mary Ann I said hi. Merry Christmas Tommy." Quaid leaned in, shaking his old friend's hand, not worrying about his trembling. He pulled out his wallet and his finger fluttered trying to grip the dollar bills, paying Judy for the Christmas supplies, but she didn't notice. He grabbed an armful of bags from the counter.

Judy lifted the other bags and followed Quaid to the truck. "What's your dog's name?"

"Rembrandt," Quaid answered, opening the driver's door. Rembrandt scooted close to the young girl, nudging his head toward her.

"Hey, you're cute," Judy offered, giving Rembrandt a pat as his tail wagged wildly. "Have a Merry Christmas, Mr. Witherspoon," she said, walking over by her dad.

"Merry Christmas, Judy. Thanks again for the help," Quaid called out getting into the driver's seat.

The old truck rattled as the motor started, moving along the curvy treed lined street headed to Gull Lane.

The truck shifted into park.

Rembrandt didn't waste any time leaping from the truck running to the side of the cottage. Quaid grabbed an armful of bags and stepped onto the porch when much to his surprise, Levi drove up and parked next to his old truck.

"Hey," Levi called, "I saw Sandy's car was gone."

"Yes, she had to go home for a few days, but she'll be back, Friday. Perfect timing, Levi. You can help me with this Christmas tree."

"No problem. Wow, you went out shopping, you're changing my friend. I see you're getting into the Christmas spirit."

"Sure am, if I can figure out this tree. I promised Sandy to get things ready for Christmas."

"It's not complicated," Levi said, grabbing ahold of the tree. "Let's put the tree in front of the picture window. It'll look nice there."

"Here's the stand," Quaid offered, handing Levi the red and green thing with legs.

"You ain't ever put up a tree?" Levi questioned, bending down holding onto the tree.

"I helped my mom when I was young, but I hired someone to decorate my condo in New York."

"Boy, you've missed out on life," Levi declared, straightening up the stand. "You mean there are really people who go around putting up Christmas trees and decorating houses for people?"

"Yes, you mean for people that are dummy's like me?" Quaid laughed.

Levi shook his head. "Okay, help me lift the tree into the stand. Keep the tree straight and turn the screws to hold it in place when I tell you. Alright," he said, pulling himself up from the old wooden floor. "Now the lights," he said, circling the tree laying the lights on the thick limbs. "Oh, I almost forgot why I stopped by. When I saw Sandy was gone, I thought I'd bring supper over tonight. Do you have some beer?"

"I have plenty of beer and a good home cooked meal sounds great," Quaid grinned, "especially one Jenny cooked."

"Good," Levi said, staring at the tree, "gotta go. I'll see you later. I have a charter at two, but I'll be back by four. Don't want to be out on the water after dark."

"Thanks for the help," Quaid yelled, plugging in the Christmas lights. He added the ornaments, being so very careful not to break them, and then he threw the silvery tinsel over the tree.

"There," he said sliding the mess of boxes into the hall closet. "I do believe this is going to be the best Christmas ever, Rembrandt. Even my mom would be proud of this tree."

Quaid opened the back door stepping out into the sunshine, and sat down in one of the rockers. Rembrandt ran past.

"Hey, where are you?" came, a voice from the kitchen.

"I'm out back."

"I'm getting me a beer," Levi said, stopping at the screen door, "do you want one?"

"Sure, how was the fishing?"

"The water was a little rough and the wind has stirred things up, but not bad. We caught a few," Levi answered, handing Quaid a beer before sitting down in the rocker next to him.

"Do you know who owns Turtle Island?" Quaid questioned, leaning over in his rocker tapping his fingers on the seat.

"The Jacob's family has owned it since the 1700's. Why?" Levi asked, squeezing his eyes tight.

"I was wondering if I could buy it."

"Buy an island," Levi shouted, stopping the rocker. "Quaid, are you nuts!"

"Sandy loves it out there and it's not big enough to do much with it, so maybe the family would sell it to me."

"You could ask Jana Ann and see if she'd check into it but I think you've gone cuckoo. I do love to go out there and fish and Jenny would love it."

"I'm going to do it," Quaid said, picking up the phone, pushing the buttons, a few to many times, but finally getting the number correct.

"Jana Ann, this is Quaid. Yes, I'm doing fine. The roast was delicious. No, I won't be able to come Christmas. I know I'd have fun, but my plans have changed. Listen, you know the small island to the south past the Marina…yes, Turtle Island. Do you think the Jacob family might consider selling the island? Yes, I'm serious! All right, slow down. Let me know, bye."

Quaid held onto the phone for a second. "She's going to check into it, but I think she thinks I'm nuts, too." He stood from the rocker, "I'm hungry. Let's see what you brought. I do like all this attention with food."

"Well, I'm not trying to win you over," Levi said, following Quaid inside the kitchen. "I'll let the women work on trying to catch you."

Quaid ignored Levi and moved over by the kitchen table.

Levi slipped a large bowl from the brown bag. "We have to put the dish in the oven for a while and let it warm up. It's some kind of casserole."

"I'm sure it's good, Jenny is a great cook just like her mom," Quaid added.

Yep and her mom still cooks the best meals."

How is Abigail doing?

"Not bad, she doesn't get around very good, but she sure can bake the finest pies."

"I need to go see her sometime."

"She'd like that. She talks about you a lot. She's so proud of you."

Levi slid the casserole into the heated oven.

"It couldn't be any easier, Jenny sure does spoil you. Come on into the living room and enjoy the tree."

"You did a great job," Levi said following Quaid. "Sandy is going to love it, but there aren't any presents under the tree."

"Give me some time. There is one thing...I'm buying," Quaid paused rubbing his finger on his left hand, "I hope goes over well."

"Quaid," Levi snapped as he sat up in his chair. "You're going to ask Sandy to marry you?"

"It's a long time coming and I hope I'm not pushing her to quickly."

"Life's too short to worry about anything. I say go for it. I was worried at first, but you're right to take a chance."

"I hope she says yes."

"I know she loves you. Jenny is going to be beside herself but I won't tell her anything until you tell me it's alright."

"Good, because it might not work out."

"It's going to be some Christmas with you buying Sandy an island and asking her to marry you. You're raising the standards around here. We mere mortals won't be able to keep up."

Quaid became quiet.

Levi sat up in his chair. "What are you really worried about?"

"I think she's hiding something and it bothers me, but I guess I'm letting my imagination run free."

"Did you find your answer about the painting?" Levi questioned. "It sure is something."

"Yes," Quaid sighed, "she was going through a divorce and it was a difficult time. I knew something had happened for her to give it up. The painting held too many memories for her to keep it. Seeing all the secret hidden messages reminded her too much of me and our summer."

"What do you mean hidden messages?"

"I did some cryptic messages about our summer together and hid them in the artwork. You have to look carefully to find the pieces."

"I knew it was shrouded with mystery."

"Yes," Quaid said, "it is, and no I'm not telling you where any of them are, it's a secret."

The old friends sat down at the kitchen table telling tall tales that had grown over the years, bringing back memories when they would hang out together without the girls, when they were young men.

Levi sighed, putting his elbows on the table, ducking his head down in his hands. "I miss the girls."

"Me, too. So much for bachelorhood," Quaid added. "I can guarantee it's not so great."

"Now," Levi stood, lifting out two pieces of homemade coconut cake from a bag on the counter, "our dessert."

"Wow!" Quaid exclaimed, "Jenny is something else."

Levi scraped his plate clean. "Well, I better get going, Jenny calls every night and we talk for a while. It helps me get through the night. We haven't been apart very often since we got married."

"I said it before and I'll say it again, you're a lucky man, Levi Sanders. Thanks for the food and tell Jenny thanks. You can tell her Sandy is spending Christmas here and I put up a tree. Oh, I also want you to come over Christmas day, when she gets home, anytime."

"I'll tell her."

125

The men stepped out onto the porch into the dark night.

"Thanks again for helping me with the tree."

"No problem, see you later, bye Rembrandt."

Quaid's back rested against the worn chair. The fresh scent of the tree brought back memories from Christmas's of the past when he was a young boy. The smells of cookies and pies baking in the kitchen would fill his home.

His mom, Louise, would sing Christmas carols as she decorated the most spectacular ten-foot tree that sat in the living room between the two large front windows. It was always perfect with silvery tinsel glistening from the glow of the big swirly lights in colors of red, green, blue, and white. Those memories of his mom having parties, singing, playing the piano, he would keep alive for the both of them, not letting one-minute escape from his mind.

Morning came quickly and Quaid leapt out of bed. He was going to the jewelry store to buy an engagement ring.

"Good morning, Rembrandt, this is going to be a busy day. Today I get to play Santa. I think I'll get Karrie and Jana Ann each a nice bottle of wine. Oh, I don't want to forget Georgina she loves chocolate candy, so a nice box of mixed chocolates will work. I think I will get Abigail a nice shawl to keep her warm.

One more gift, something special for Jenny." He walked around the bedroom and squatted down on the floor next to one of the boxes full of small paintings sitting against the wall. As he searched through the paintings, his past was staring him in his face, paintings he hadn't touched in years. His hands pulled out a painting of a lone fishing boat swaying out on the blue water.

"This is perfect."

Quaid sat leaning back against the wall gripping the painting in his hands, seeing memories flow through his mind of when he painted the small piece. Each of his paintings was like his children, knowing the exact time they were created.

"Jenny will love this painting as much as I do," he said to Rembrandt.

Jenny and Quaid's friendship began when they were young becoming good friends over the years. Jenny's mother, Abigail worked for the Witherspoon's at the three-story home on the beach.

Jenny was Quaid's biggest fan, always encouraging him, especially since she had a passion for art and dreamed of drawing great masterpieces like him. Days and days, he would sit patiently teaching her to draw.

Their love they had for each other was unique, special, even Levi never could understand. He was envious at first of Quaid, but learned to let the jealousy go. Jenny was an excellent artist, but getting married and having children was her true passion, along with her love for Levi.

Quaid's hands trembled, holding the painting out in front of him. This was the perfect gift. His paintings had become so precious to him since there would never be anymore. His excitement grew. This was going to be the greatest Christmas.

He finished his shower, pulling on a clean pair of jeans, a shirt, and clean socks.

He stopped at the front door. He pulled in a deep breath, going to the hardware store was one thing, but going to a jewelry store was a lot for him. He didn't have any other choice; he wasn't going to let Sandy down. Here, he had moved to the cottage to hide away, but now he would be out among people. He grabbed his jacket from the hook on the kitchen wall by the back door. It was time to leave.

Gull Lane curved back and forth following along the coast into the small town of Hathaway Cove, which was bustling with people darting in and out of stores. Christmas music flowed from speakers attached to the old brick buildings, resonating down the long street. The town was dressed in its finest with twinkling lights and big red bows along with greenery wrapped on all the light poles.

Hathaway Cove was a quaint, old fashion town right out of a book of Rockwell paintings, maybe that was another reason Quaid was drawn back. He loved the diagonal parking and his luck was holding out finding a parking spot right in front of the jewelry store.

Quaid took in a deep breath, getting out of the truck. He smiled knowing the news would get around quickly about him being in the jewelry store. He chuckled to himself. All the women would be speculating about which one would be receiving the Christmas gift and what the gift could be.

He pushed open the jewelry store door it chimed.

"Good morning," the woman behind the counter said, looking at him through thick glasses. "How can I help you?"

"I'm looking for an engagement ring."

"Oh, my," she said excitedly, "They're right here."

"The ring in the back of the case is magnificent."

"This ring," the woman offered lifting the ring out of the case, "is called *forever,* and has the largest diamond. It the best quality we have. The clarity is amazing."

Quaid stood, his hands in his pockets, staring down at the ring sparkling so beautifully, sitting in its blue velvet box on the counter.

"I'll take it." He walked around the glass case studying what was inside. "Do you also have some unique necklaces?"

"Over here," the chubby woman declared, swishing to the side counter.

"The necklace second row from the back is different," Quaid said curiously.

"The necklace is called *sand and waves,*" the woman answered, lifting up the silver necklace.

The necklace sparkled in the light. Quaid wanted to hold the necklace, but kept his hands to his side. The necklace had a silver pendent hanging down in a long wave with specks of silver along it. The jeweler had captured the sand in a distinctive way, the same as Quaid had always tried.

"I'll take that as well. Can you wrap it for me in Christmas paper?"

"Sure," the woman said eagerly, "not a problem." The small box became covered in silver with dark blue stars and the woman meticulously tied a matching blue ribbon on top in a beautiful bow.

Quaid handed the woman his credit card and she laid down his receipt on the glass counter. His body tensed when he gripped the pen letting his hand twitch wildly scribbling his name. He felt the woman's stare. He looked up seeing her face tightening into a frown looking at his signature.

"Aren't you the famous artist that lives in Miss. Eula's cottage?"

"Yes," he said grinning. For one of the first times in years he was enjoying the look on the woman's face staring at his hands.

"Alright," Quaid exclaimed, laying all of his purchases on the floor of the truck. "We need to go to the hardware," he said, looking over at Rembrandt. "We have to get Amos and Levi their gifts."

The truck bounced into the gravel parking lot of the hardware. Quaid stepped out of the truck and Rembrandt quickly stuck his head out the window.

"Good morning, Quaid. Need some more ornaments?" Tommy asked, standing over to the side by the Christmas trees.

"Nope, I need some gifts."

"Hi, Mr. Witherspoon. You can let Rembrandt out of the truck, he won't bother anything," Judy offered, hurrying to the truck door.

"If you say so," Quaid said, looking over at Tommy as the short, gray-haired man shook his head yes.

Rembrandt leapt from the truck scooting close to Judy as she bent down to rub his ears and head.

"Come on in, Quaid," Tommy said, waving his arm in the air going through the doorway. "What is it you're looking for?"

"I need to get Amos and Levi some fishing tackle."

"We got some new stuff in last week. Come on back and take a look."

Quaid followed his old friend back into the store, smelling mustiness and fertilizer.

"Oh," Quaid stopped walking standing next to the dog supplies. "I forgot to get Rembrandt a Christmas present."

"You can get him some treats. This toy is also fun. All the dogs seem to like it."

"Shampoo," Quaid said, picking up a bottle and reading it. "Is it hard to give a dog a bath?"

Tommy started laughing. "It depends on the dog, but Rembrandt will let you do anything. He's a great animal."

"Well," Quaid sighed, "then he needs a bath for Christmas. He smells." Quaid stared at all the fishing equipment hanging on the back wall. "Wow, you carry a lot of fishing gear."

"We sure do," Tommy said, walking over by him. "I see some confusion in your face."

"I want something that Amos and Levi wouldn't buy for themselves, a special gift for both."

"Well…this is it," Tommy assured, picking up some tackle. "This stuff is brand new and those boys wouldn't spend this kind of money on themselves. But they'd sure dream about buying it."

"Then it's the perfect gift."

Rembrandt lay on the floor by the door watching Judy wrap the gifts.

"Judy," Quaid asked, "can you put some wrapping paper and a nice bow in the sack. I have one gift at home to wrap."

"Sure, no problem, Mr. Witherspoon," Judy said, putting a beautiful red bow, some ribbon and some paper on the counter.

Tommy lifted the brown sack off the counter. Judy grabbed his arm. "Daddy, wait a second." She placed another small gift in the bag with a big grin on her face.

Quaid pulled the truck door open. Judy bent down hugging Rembrandt. She laughed. "He sure does need the shampoo. Merry Christmas, Mr. Witherspoon and Rembrandt."

A Faded Cottage

"Merry Christmas to you both," Quaid called out, his arm waving goodbye out the window.

Quaid stacked the gifts around the tree placing the one gift from Judy to Rembrandt near the back of the tree for Christmas morning. "Now the tree looks nice."

Quaid laid the Christmas paper Judy had given him on the kitchen table. He carefully placed the painting of the boat on top. The paper pulled together, but his hands were trembling and it was a hit and miss, as his fingers were fumbling trying to tape the paper together. He sighed with disgust wrapping the red ribbon around the box tying the ribbon in a bow; a child would have done a better job.

He shook his head knowing Jenny wouldn't mind the flaws in the wrapped gift, but it still irritated him. He sat the present underneath the tree near the back.

He grabbed his worn jacket from the hook. He sat down in the old rocker and unhurriedly pushed it back and forth. He looked over at Rembrandt; this week had been a whirlwind. Just a few days ago, he was all alone hiding from everyone, a sorry old man, but now he felt alive.

The evening moved on quietly as he stood on the back porch watching Rembrandt run around the side of the cottage. Quaid could see the Atlantic Ocean heaving with large motion like it was breathing far out on the horizon. The air was getting chilly, making him shudder. Another cold front would be moving in soon.

Later that night he climbed into the bed, deep under the covers, with Rembrandt lying down at the foot. "One more day and she'll be back," he whispered, letting the pillow swallow his head.

DIANN SHADDOX

A Faded Cottage

Buying a Dream

The next morning Quaid went through his daily routine, slipping on his jeans, eating his breakfast, getting ready for the day.

"Today's Thursday, we need to get everything ready for Sandy," he said, looking down at Rembrandt.

His phone began to ring. "Hello, Jana Ann. Yes, I was up. You're the best. Yes, this afternoon will be fine. I have a couple of errands to run this morning. See you later, thanks."

Quaid stood in front of the bathroom mirror, his bushy eyebrows lifted up. He laughed, as he played with his long hair able to put it into a ponytail. He had dealt with the stares when he was out shopping, so why not deal with a barber. He watched as his head twitched from side to side. He finally laughed he was saying no all the time.

Quaid picked up the grocery list. First a haircut and a beard trim then Piggly Wiggly for groceries.

Right after lunch he heard a car out front and he hurriedly opened the door. Jana Ann marched into the room on a mission. Her high heels tapped on the wood floor, a big grin covering her face.

"See what you think," she exclaimed, quickly handing him the papers.

His reading glasses shifted on his face reading the paper in front of him. "This is amazing."

"Yes," she answered, standing proud, arching her shoulders looking up into his eyes. "You need to sign the papers where I've marked." Her body leaned in close to his.

He held onto the papers and moved away from her. Having peering eyes made his hands tremble worse. His hand tried to grip the pen, but Jana Ann wasn't deterred. She stepped up getting even closer to him. His hands shook in a wild frenzy, as he tried to turn his body away from her.

Quaid laid the back of his hand down on the desk gripping the pen very tightly, squeezing his fingers together, scribbling his name, again not the writing of a famed artist. He turned around handing the papers back to her.

Jana Ann didn't move. He slid pass her and hurried to the Christmas tree. He picked up the bottle of wine wrapped in a festive sack with elves and Santa's all over.

"Merry Christmas, Jana Ann," he announced. "Thank you for helping me the past few months."

"Merry Christmas, Quaid." She took a deep breath holding onto the wrapped bottle of wine. He could see in her eyes she'd heard about the trip to the jewelry store.

"Thanks, Jana Ann," he lifted up the tray of dishes, "for the roast."

"You're welcome, Quaid," she said gratefully. She opened the car door, letting him put the clanking tray in the back seat. "I hope you find what you're looking for, Quaid," she said softly, staring up at him.

"Bye, Jana Ann." He stepped back from the car, letting her slide into the driver seat, quickly closing the door. "Call and let me know when I need to finalize the papers."

"Congratulations on buying Turtle Island Merry Christmas," she called out.

"Merry Christmas," he shouted, watching her drive away.

"All right, boy." Quaid leaned down, petting Rembrandt. "We now own Turtle Island," he said shaking his head, "what a week."

He slowly walked around the cottage. "This place is a mess. I need to do something with the boxes in the bedroom."

The old wooden steps creaked as he made his way up the stairs. He sat box after box on the floor in the corner of the guest bedroom and laughed. Out of sight, out of mind.

He opened the French doors in the upstairs bedroom and fresh air filled his lungs when he stepped outside. He smiled to himself. There to the side were two chase lounges and a small table, a perfect place for Sandy to lie out in the sun.

Sitting down in one of the lounge chairs, his head rested against the back of the chair. His eyes closed hearing the waves serenade him. He didn't move for a while lying there in a rare state of relaxation.

Please let Sandy want to stay here with me. I promise I won't complain about my tremors or my life.

His eyes opened when a soft breeze blew, lightly touching his face. He sat up in the chair staring out at the water. He could see boats on the horizon looking so tiny in the scheme of the grand water, as if they were toys in a bathtub.

His life was like the tiny specks bouncing around in the water looking for some justice in the unjust world. The old saying when one door closes another door can open was working for him. He had lost his ability to paint great masterpieces, but he had found his true love.

"You know, Rembrandt, I've lived all over the world. I lived one summer in Paris and one summer in a small town near Rome, Italy and traveled all over Europe. I've painted my paintings from some of the most beautiful places on this earth. I've stayed on Fuji for months and lived six months in Australia, but nothing compares to sitting right here looking at the great Atlantic from my own faded cottage. I kept trying to find my perfect spot in the world, traveling to different countries. Turns out I'd already discovered my paradise. I was too stubborn to understand or maybe I was afraid to admit I'd failed at something in my life. Not now, ole boy, I'm not letting this dream slip through my fingers, not again."

His housecleaning chores done, Quaid scanned the cottage, proud of himself. Sandy always loved everything in its place.

The contract lay on top of the Christmas paper on the kitchen table. The Christmas paper flapped like a bird's wings. He sighed. Getting irritated wasn't going to help; he'd try to wrap the envelope later.

He went to the kitchen, poured himself a glass of wine, and sat down in his rocker on the back porch. It was his way of relaxing watching the setting sun with its brilliant colors swirling in the heavens reflecting down upon the water. Clouds were growing in the east, but it wasn't a bad day for the twenty-third of December. His eyes closed listening to the lone seagull squawking finding his fish, the unseen journey of our existence.

Later in the evening, his hands calmed and he was able to wrap the contract. He placed the last present under the tree, laying it right in the front. Christmas music began to flow throughout the cottage and Quaid sang softly with some of the old songs, bringing Christmas to life.

His hands clinched together and his left hand wiggled. Maybe he'd have a ring on his finger sooner than later. He shook his head back and forth, wondering if his life could truly become perfect. But worry still lingered in the back of his mind. What was Sandy's secret?

A Faded Cottage

The Power of Love

Quaid's body shook waking himself from a night of wonderful dreams. He sat up in bed. He had so much energy. "Christmas Eve," his voice rose with delight.

He hopped out of bed, tugging the sheets from the bed. He showered, put on some clean jeans and a fresh washed shirt, slipping on his tennis shoes. He chuckled checking his socks. Rembrandt was even moving quicker this morning. It was as if he knew Sandy was coming home.

He scooped out the ashes in the fireplace preparing fresh wood for a fire tonight. The Christmas tree lights shined brightly, all their colors bouncing against the walls. Everything was perfect. He walked through the house, back and forth, unable to sit still. His body throbbed with anticipation. He couldn't even eat his lunch since his stomach was churning.

Crunching of the rocks out front made his heart stop. He tried to breathe, taking in a deep breath, hurrying to the door, believing he was going to hyperventilate…

The front door swung open and standing on the porch was Sandy. She ran to him putting her arms around his neck, pulling him close. They kissed, not moving until Rembrandt pushed his nose in between them wanting a pat.

Sandy laughed. "Wow, boy you smell nice," she said, kneeling down, hugging the dog with her head lying next to his.

"We boys...cleaned up," Quaid said, smiling proud with his playful grin.

"I see you did, Merry Christmas," she said, letting her fingers rub through Quaid's trimmed hair. "We need to unload my car, it's full. I brought a lot of food, but I also brought a lot of clothes," she confessed, not looking at Quaid, turning her head back to the car. Quaid smiled. She was nervous.

Quaid's heart started pumping, hurrying out the car knowing she was staying. The car was finally unloaded and the last box of food sat on the kitchen table.

"I put the presents under the tree."

"Those are for tomorrow morning so no peeking, either one of you," she giggled. "I made chowder, but I didn't make the rest of the food. Pam, a friend of mine who loves to cook, made a great Christmas dinner for us along with some extra homemade rolls and pies. We won't starve."

Sandy paused for a second, looking around the room. "I don't see any dishes around here. What happened to your lady friends?"

"I guess they got busy," Quaid answered, shrugging his shoulders with a big grin spreading across his face.

"Let's see if we can find room in the refrigerator for all of this," she said, looking back at him.

"Did you eat any lunch?" he questioned, looking at how pale she was. If it was possible, she'd grown thinner in just a week.

"I grabbed a hamburger on my way down. I'm fine," she assured, gently placing her hand on his face. "Stop worrying."

138

"I put your clothes in the bedroom. Yesterday, I cleaned out some space in the closet and the chest for your things."

"Good, I'll put the rest of my clothes away later," she answered relieved he was excited as she was. "Let's go for a walk when I finish with the food. I know it is a little cold out, but nice."

Sandy stood at the kitchen table emptying the last sack of food. She meticulously folded the sacks, laying them in the pantry. The pantry door closed and she walked to the back door.

"Wait a minute," Quaid called to her. "Come over here. I want you to open one of your gifts," he exclaimed excitedly.

"We need to wait until morning to open our gifts," she declared, following him into the living room.

"Just one gift," he added, sitting down on the ottoman in front of the tree, pulling the present out.

"Oh, the tree is beautiful. Did you decorate it?"

"Yes," he said proudly, "but Levi assisted."

"It smells so fresh. You did a great job," she assured, looking at all of the ornaments. "I especially love the seashells and seagull ornaments."

"Here," he said fidgeting, handing her the present he'd wrapped last night.

She sat down on the ottoman, scooting over by him.

He pulled in a sigh. "I wrapped it," he confessed.

She lay the present in her lap, reaching over taking his hands in her hands holding them tenderly.

He sighed as he relaxed.

Sandy pulled off the Christmas paper and lifted up the yellow envelope. "What's this?" The stack of papers slid out of the envelope and she began to read. "You bought Turtle Island?" she screamed!

"Yes, I did. We own Turtle Island. It's yours to do what you want with it. You can mess with all the plants and no one can ever bother them, just as you always wished."

139

Tears ran down her face. "Quaid," she sniffed. "You actually spent this much money...for an island.

Rembrandt nudged her, worriedly.

"Yes, it's what you always dreamed about. It was your wish to be able to take care of Turtle Island. I'm going to try and give you everything you've ever wished for." He reached in kissing her gently, wiping her tears of joy. "Let's go for our walk and soon we'll go back to Turtle Island."

Sandy grabbed him laying her head next to his chest. She then laid the papers on the desk grabbing her jacket.

Quaid held the screen door and Rembrandt ran past. She wrapped her arm around Quaid and they walked out onto the porch.

"It's so nice out," she announced, stopping on the boardwalk. "It's hard to believe today is Christmas Eve. This Christmas is going to be wonderful."

"Yes, it is, the best Christmas ever. I got Amos, Georgina, Abigail, Levi, and Jenny gifts. I told Levi to bring Jenny over tomorrow afternoon when she comes home from Braelyn's. I hope it was alright?"

"I'd love to see Jenny, it's been too long." Sandy stopped walking. "You know, the reason I didn't contact them when I would visit the cottage was," her head ducked down not looking at him. "They made me think of you. I always knew how much you cared for Jenny. I guess I was jealous."

"You, like Levi, never need to be jealous of Jenny. Our friendship is a great friendship and will always be. I guess you could say she's like my little sister, we're so much alike."

"I know how much she loves Levi, but it was too difficult to see them without you," she answered, looking out to the water. "You were always with them. It was hard to think about the past. They reminded me of what I had missed."

He stopped walking and reached his arm around her, pulling her close, looking into her eyes. "You don't have to ever be without me, not anymore," he whispered, feeling her softly breathing, not wanting to let her go.

"Oh, this is the best Christmas I've ever had. I feel like a kid. I can't believe it's Christmas Eve," she confessed, pushing away from him, swirling around in a circle.

Their walk continued, but Sandy was getting tired and the air was getting colder. She shivered and he brought her close. They headed back to the cottage seeing the storm growing out in the Atlantic Ocean.

Quaid lit the fire in the fireplace and turned on the Christmas music. Sandy put the chowder on the stove to warm and the rolls in the oven.

He sat down in his chair with the lights from the tree glistening colors, flickering on the walls around the room.

The timer in the kitchen beeped and Sandy dipped the chowder into their bowls. The meal was extraordinary, but Quaid just went through the motions of eating.

Sandy settled into the chair in front of the fire. The Christmas music played quietly in the room and the lights twinkled in a soft glow.

He walked slowly from the kitchen trying to think what he was going to say. Quaid got down on one knee. His hand reached out to Sandy, gently holding her hand, but the words didn't come. He opened the blue velvet box showing her the sparkling ring. His hands and body were shaking, but not from the tremors.

Sandy chuckled lovingly. "Quaid Witherspoon, what are you doing?"

He did a big swallow. "I'm trying to ask you to marry me. Oh, the words didn't come out right. I'm messing everything up," he sighed, his eyebrows squeezed together.

"You're fine," she whispered, laying her hand on his shoulders, "but first, I need to talk to you before I answer." She looked down at the ring. "This is the most beautiful ring. You don't make things easy."

He moaned.

"Now stop, calm down. I'm not saying no, give a girl a few minutes. I need to talk to you. Sit
down in your chair and try to relax before you pass out. Take a deep breath, but breathe slowly."

His body quivered sitting back in his chair as she began to talk.

"I don't know how to say this," she began in a soft voice, turning her head from him looking at the tree, tears welling in her eyes. "I have a heart defect."

His body leaped from the chair, his eyes wide. "What!"

"I was born with a hole in my heart," she said as she squeezed her arms together, looking back into those blue eyes full of fear.

"How could you live with a hole in your heart?"

"It was small and the doctors believed I was fine for years, but…"

"But, what," Quaid interrupted.

"A few months ago, I began to have problems. My doctor decided I needed surgery. The surgery went well, but I just found out a few days ago I developed an infection. I've been in the hospital the last few days."

"An infection!"

"Yes. I'm on medications."

"What are you saying?"

"Next week I'm going in for another surgery to repair a leak in my heart valve.

"Then you're going to be fine?"

She shook her head no. "The odds aren't good."

"What?" he yelled. He couldn't breathe. "We'll get the best doctors!"

"I have the best doctors and I'm not done yet so please calm down."

"Why didn't you tell me this last weekend?"

"I didn't want to interfere with our special day. I wanted to give us some time together without worry."

He sat down on the ottoman nearest her. "We'll get through this. You'll be fine. We'll have years together. Stop worrying about me. I can help you."

"I have to worry about you, adding this burden on," her eyes dropped to the floor. "It's not fair," she whispered, sniffing.

"Life's not fair, but with us fighting together, you'll be alright." He stared into those green eyes and leaned close. "My answer?" He whispered.

"You're such a little boy. Yes! I'll marry you, Quaid Witherspoon."

"Yes!" He yelled, jumping into the air.

Rembrandt barked.

"Alright, we have to plan the wedding and soon."

"You don't want to wait to see about my surgery and if it works?" She tightened her lips, "We have to be prepared."

"No, we're not waiting," he exclaimed. "The sooner the better. This has been my dream and nothing is going to stop us." He squatted down next to her. "Choose a day next week."

"I need to look at the weather. I want to get married on the beach and it has to be a pretty day."

"Okay," he agreed, flipping the channels finding the local news.

They sat patiently as the newscaster talked and talked, but finally the weather came on.

"Friday is going to be wonderful, New Year's Eve. Do you think we can get everything done by then?"

"I know someone at city hall, Karrie. She'll help and Jenny will be home tomorrow. She'll get the wedding done hell or high water," he said, laughing. He sat on the ottoman stroking her hands, pulling her to him.

"We're getting married," he said it repeatedly as her hand gently rubbed his face. "We don't have to stay up. I want you to get plenty of rest."

"Look!" she screamed, letting her hands drop from his face. "They're saying it might snow Sunday. I can't believe they're talking about snow!"

She relaxed, letting her tired body fall back into the cushioned chair.

"I see how exhausted you are." He was so worried seeing her face had become even lighter in color.

"I'm fine, this is resting enough for me, but we do have to go to bed so Santa can come and leave our gifts," she said softly. "This is Christmas Eve."

"Santa is going to make our dreams come true," he assured. "We're going to have years together.

She pulled the sparkling ring from the velvet box, slipping it on her finger. "It fits perfectly. Look," she squealed. "Its colors are so radiant with the reflections from the tree and fire making it sparkle. I've never had anything so beautiful. Quaid," she paused, "is this truly happening? Are we getting married?"

"Yes," he whispered, leaning over kissing her. "All your dreams are going to become a reality, wait and see."

"I thought I was always the positive one. Merry Christmas, Quaid," she whispered, getting comfortable in her chair. She closed her eyes, falling asleep.

A Faded Cottage

Lost Letters

Quaid sat in his chair in front of the crackling fire letting Sandy sleep, not wanting to disturb her, taking in every feature of her tired but beautiful face. This was more than he could take - a heart problem. He had thought she had someone else in her life, not an infection that might take her away. How trivial he felt worried about his own feelings.

He shook his head. God couldn't be so cruel to let them have only a few days then take her away, could he? His trembling hands gripped into fists. Once again fate was taking over and he didn't know how to stop it. Tears began to fall down his face, but he wasn't going to let her see. He kept his head turned toward the Christmas tree just in case she woke. He couldn't lose her, not now. He could see by the light of the fire how pale she was. One week and then she'd have her surgery. Quaid prayed the surgery would work and they'd live to grow old together, sitting right here in this cottage on Gull Lane. He had to believe. He couldn't think of the alternative. Life without her.

Time moved on and he gently woke Sandy. "It's time for bed," he whispered.

She looked up at him with her tired green eyes.

He climbed into bed next to her, snuggling her closely as she fell right back to sleep, exhausted from the busy day.

****

He woke early Christmas day. He lay in the bed for a few minutes watching her sleep, seeing Sandy's beautiful, pale face blend with the white of the pillowcase. He couldn't sleep, a tightening in his throat was making it difficult for him to breathe. He lifted up the quilt slowly and climbed out of bed. His mind wouldn't let him rest.

He lit a fire in the fireplace warming the room, sitting down in his overstuffed chair, cupping his mug of coffee in his hands. His eyes stayed mesmerized as he watched the lights flicker on the Christmas tree.

"Good morning and Merry Christmas," Sandy called out, coming into the living room. "The fire feels good." She scooted close to the fireplace, turning her butt to the fire as she shivered.

"Merry Christmas," he called to her, jumping out of his chair, "do you want a cup of coffee?"

"Yes, but I can get it."

"No, you sit down. I'm going to take care of you," he insisted.

"Quaid, I still can do things."

"I know, but you're taking it easy for a while. You have a wedding to plan," he chuckled, pouring her a fresh cup of coffee. "Are you ready for gifts?"

She laughed. "I'm ready."

He handed her the small silver box and she slowly began to pull the paper off.

"Oh, this is beautiful, but Quaid, you've done enough. An island and an engagement ring and now a necklace?"

"The necklace is called *sand and waves*."

A Faded Cottage

"It's beautiful, I can see the sand and waves," she whispered, lifting it up, placing it around her neck, carefully closing the clasp.

"Here, Rembrandt," Quaid said, laying Judy's gift in front of him, "it's ok boy, the gift is yours, it's from Judy at the hardware." Rembrandt looked down at the reindeer paper and began to rip the paper with his teeth, holding onto the gift with his paw. Lying in front of the dog was a stuffed animal which he quickly began chewing, letting the toy squeak.

Sandy and Rembrandt opened the rest of their gifts, one after another.

"Quaid, it's your turn, you need to pull out the blue gift with Santa's all over it and open it first," Sandy announced, leaning over, picking up the paper around her chair.

Quaid lifted up the present, slowly tearing off the wrapping paper. An expensive set of paints and brushes was lying in front of him. "Sandy, this is nice, but I can't use them."

She moved over to him and sat down on the arm of the chair, gently putting her hand on his shoulder. "Yes you can. You're going to give it a chance and let go of your pride. You love to paint and I want you to paint for me, not for anyone else, just like you used to do. Let your hands shake. Don't try and do such tedious work. Let your hands move freely."

He picked up the other big boxes and tore the paper off each of them. In front of him were new canvases and an easel.

"After we get dressed, we're making you a studio upstairs in the guest bedroom. That room has the best light in the cottage. You can even sit outside on the porch and paint when it's warm."

He pulled her into his lap. "You understand I can't ever say no to you, but I still don't know about trying to paint again. My paintings will be scribbled, not precise."

"You and I don't give up on anything. I'm not worried if your paintings aren't perfect. Please try again for me," she said tenderly, rubbing the back of his neck.

"Alright," he whispered, bringing her face to his.

She pulled herself back out of the chair. "I'm hungry. I think I'll have a piece of pumpkin pie for breakfast."

He looked at her. "You need something better than pie."

She pouted and he laughed.

"Alright, let's get some breakfast or whatever you call it. Of course, it could be our lunch by the time we get done. We should probably get our showers since I don't know when Jenny and Levi might stop by."

Sandy finished her piece of pie hurriedly, took her shower, and dressed, ready to get to work empting her suitcases. Everything had to be in correct order.

"Let's go upstairs," she announced, closing the drawers in the chest.

"If you say so," he answered hesitantly.

He picked up the paints and canvases and carried them with him.

She followed right behind him. She stepped into the bedroom and laughed.

"So this is where all your stuff went? I wondered how you cleaned things up so well."

"I didn't know where to put everything," he answered sheepishly, shrugging his shoulders. "I thought this was a perfect place."

"I'll get things straightened up in here," she laughed. "You get everything prepared to paint. We can move the bed next to the wall. I want you to be by the windows. The windows up here are amazing," she added, standing and looking out into the ocean. "I might have to join you when it warms up. I do love to lie out in the sun it energizes me. I also, might put a two piece bathing suit on."

"You do know how to entice someone to paint. I agree this room has the perfect light," he said straightening up his brushes.

"Oh, Quaid," she called out, opening one box of his paintings, "these are amazing." She lifted one of the paintings from the box. "I think we should hang these all over the house. Let me see, this one should go downstairs in the bedroom," she added, pulling out painting after painting.

"I gave Jenny a painting like the one you have out, a picture of a lone boat out in the sea. I hope she likes it."

"You don't have to worry, she loves your work. It will be the greatest Christmas present for her. Is this all of your painting or do you have more?"

"I have many paintings in New York, but these are some of my favorites, some of the smaller ones I did years ago."

"It's alright to hang them, isn't it?" she asked, worried she'd overstepped her boundaries by pulling out the paintings.

"You pick all the ones you want and I'll hang them later."

She was like a kid in a candy store.

"I'll pick a few and then we can go downstairs and hang them. I also need to put some of the food in the oven since some of the dishes have to warm for a while."

Her hands eagerly reached into another box, selecting more of the paintings of the beach and Turtle Island.

Her hands stopped moving. Down in one of the old boxes were some pieces of folded paper crushed between two paintings. She lifted the crumpled papers out of the box, slowly unfolding them.

There in front of her were letters addressed to her. Her body froze as she began to read. Quaid stayed busy in the room unpacking his paints, not noticing her soft sniffles or the tears building in her eyes.

December 18th, 1952

Dear Sandy,

It's finally quiet here at my home in New York and I'm sitting on my window seat in my bedroom staring out into the dark night, not even half as beautiful, as looking out my bedroom window in the old three-story house on the beach. The lights of the city have consumed the stars not letting them shine, but the moon is full and bright, not enabling the streetlights to win.

DIANN SHADDOX

I feel so lonely. I keep painting each and every hour of the day and it seems to help deter my mind from thoughts of what could be. I shouldn't be writing this. You made your decision and I promised in the letter to abide by it, but it hasn't been easy.

I hope your life is a happy one and I will continue with mine, but thoughts of our island keep flowing and I continue to put my dreams, our dreams, on the canvas one after another. I will always have our summer in my paintings. I won't ever forget the soft warm breezes, stepping into the cool water, running and playing in the sand and of course the fishing shack and the best thing of all--holding you in my arms.

Mom wants me to go with them in a few days to the old three-story house on the beach for Christmas, but I can't. I want to relive our memories in my mind and not have them erased by the waves on the beach. I'm sorry, but I can't face you. I'm a coward, my emotions would be overflowing, and I couldn't abide by my promise.

The brilliant colors of the world are my canvases to keep you and our one summer alive, letting the memory stay etched in my mind to hold onto for eternity. I can feel your soft skin touching mine, your sweet lips, and I can see those green eyes so full of energy and joy. I think of you each waking moment of my life from early dawn as I'm watching the sunrise to dusk and then dark, when the nights are filled with stars. Our stars.

I see a shooting star flashing through the sky right at this moment, just like the one we saw on the beach late that wonderful night on Turtle Island. Believing it's an omen, a sign of our love. I now make my final wish. No matter where my life takes me, I will always love you and you will forever be a part of my life, if merely in my paintings. So my love, I will say goodnight. Sandy, I love you for all time.

Quaid

A Faded Cottage

Tears ran down her cheek and Quaid turned from the window. "Sandy, what's wrong? Are you sick?" He exclaimed, sliding down on the floor next to her.

"No," she sniffed, holding up the letter."

"I thought I threw those letters away," he said pulling her to him. "I'm sorry, they're making you cry."

The next letter she unfolded and began to read without saying anything.

December 24th, 1952
Dear Sandy,
The night is dark and peaceful. The huge grandfather clock is striking twelve. I guess it's now Christmas day. The tree is sparkling with ornaments and brilliant colors standing in the living room as I sit, alone. The fireplace is crackling with the last log being eaten as its light flickers across the presents, the ones my mom left for me under the Christmas tree. One gift lying under the tree is a small, dark blue box I bought special for you. I guess I was dreaming, hoping our fairytale would live on.

Mom and the family did go to the beach and I'm here at home, by myself. I wish Santa would arrive and bring you as my present. Then all my dreams and wishes would come true. I know I may never hold you or sit next to you again on the beach, but in my heart, you will always be near. I close my eyes and each moment of our summer flows in my mind. I will never let one second escape.

I sip my wine, making me vulnerable to my memories. The eggnog and bourbon hasn't helped to take the pain away. Again, I shouldn't be writing you this letter, but the bourbon and wine isn't stopping my hands from continuing. First, I want to say Merry Christmas. I won't forget our promise to be together this Christmas, the beginning of many of our dreams.

A new year will embark soon and we'll be on our new journeys, the start of our new lives separate from each other. I do hope you've

151

found someone and my Christmas wish for you will be always to be happy. The Christmas music is fading away, but my memories of our time together will always stay fresh in my mind and in my paintings. I will never forget.

Merry Christmas and have a wonderful life, my sweet love. I will love you for all time.

Quaid

"Why didn't you mail them?" She exclaimed.

"I promised in the one letter not to bother you, but Christmas was so difficult for me, reliving what we'd dreamed about. I kept painting and I guess the letters were put away along with the paintings about our summer."

"I have my letters now and the paintings, and the best part," she said softly, reaching over, pulling him to her hugging him tight. "I have you."

"For all time, just as the letters say. Now we need to go downstairs and hang some pictures," he said earnestly, lifting her up off the floor.

Their bodies squeezed together.

She reached up gently, touching his face. "This is our Christmas, just a few years late," she whispered, holding onto one of the paintings.

"No more tears," he added, picking up a couple of the paintings and following her down the stairs.

"Oh, don't worry, those weren't sad tears but tears of love," she replied, holding snug to the letters. She leaned the paintings against the walls all around the house, exactly where she wanted Quaid to hang them.

She turned the knob on the oven and it began to heat. The food began to warm and the house smelled as if she had been cooking Christmas dinner all morning. The turkey and dressing were warming along with the yams and green bean casserole, everything perfect.

Quaid sat at the table watching her move around the kitchen getting everything prepared. He couldn't slow her down and her face was becoming paler.

"Come on," she said with energy, not deterring with her plan, going to the laundry room to get the hammer and picture hangers. "Let's hang some of these painting."

He followed her as she went from room to room. She carefully lifted up each painting and stood measuring, and squinching her face, getting each of the pictures hung impeccably. She stood back. "They're perfect." She spun around. "This is," she said pulling him to her, "now our home."

The doorbell rang and she let go of Quaid, hurrying into the living room. The door opened wide. Standing in front of her was Levi and Jenny. Jenny's mouth flew open without words as Sandy grabbed her. "Merry Christmas, come in!"

Quaid walked into the living room and Jenny finally found her voice. "This was my dream since the summer when we were young. This is the best Christmas present ever, seeing you together."

"Congratulations on the grandbaby. What's its name?" Sandy questioned.

"Abigail, "Jenny said, "She's beautiful, named after her great-grandmother."

"Well, she has to be beautiful; we wouldn't think anything less for you girl." Quaid stepped up and hugged his old friend. "You know, I'm the one person who has known you since you were a tiny baby like baby Abigail," he said smiling.

"Yes, only a few years ago," Jenny teased. "Who is this?" Jenny asked, looking down at the dog on the rug by the fireplace.

"This is Rembrandt," Quaid grinned. "He came for visit and decided to stay. I guess he's a part of the family, now."

"Hello, Rembrandt. I'm," she paused, "your Aunt Jenny." They all laughed. She bent down petting the dog as he looked up with those brown eyes.

"Do you want any eggnog?" Sandy questioned.

"Yes," Levi said, "but I can't have any bourbon today. I have to drive to Charleston late tonight to pick up Kevin. He's coming home today from Lebanon. You know the army puts them on any flight they can and he has a late one."

"Wow! Things are going good then," Quaid patted Levi on the back.

"Looks like for both of us," Levi insisted.

"Sit down," Jenny told the men. "Sandy and I will get the eggnog. It smells good in the house. You must have learned to cook."

"Not me, a friend did all the cooking. Hey, you guys want to stay and eat? We have plenty." Sandy offered stopping in the doorway. "Jenny, we don't have to do anything but put it on the table."

"You sure," Jenny asked, "we didn't come for Christmas dinner."

"Have you eaten?" Quaid called out.

"No," Levi confirmed quickly. "I'm hungry. And I'm not bashful."

"Let's have a drink then we'll get things prepared," Sandy said, going into the kitchen.

"Sandy!" Jenny screamed.

"What's the matter?" Levi yelled, jumping out of his chair.

"Sandy's wearing a big engagement ring!" Jenny called out.

Levi sat back down in the chair.

The men laughed.

"You didn't tell her, did you?" Quaid said.

"Nope. And I forgot to ask when we came in if it was all right," Levi added, amused.

The girls sat the drinks down on the table and scooted in on the ottomans by the men.

"When is the wedding and where?" Jenny questioned.

"The wedding is this Friday, New Year's Eve," Quaid informed her, sipping his eggnog, pulling Sandy close.

"New Year's Eve? Perfect! Where are you going to have the wedding?" Jenny continued questioning.

"We're getting married on the beach, right here, late morning. It's supposed to be a beautiful day," Sandy proclaimed, lying back against Quaid.

"We have some work to do. There will be a lot to see to, but we'll get it done. We have a lot of plans to make."

"Did you know it's supposed to snow tomorrow?" Sandy added.

"Snow? You're crazy," Levi replied.

"Nope," Quaid agreed. "She's right, they're calling for snow."

"Kevin is going to love the snow," Jenny said happily.

"Oh," Quaid began, "there's something you don't know." He grinned, getting excited. "Sandy and I will officially own Turtle Island soon. Jana Ann came through with a good offer and I signed off on it."

"What!" Jenny screamed, leaning over by Quaid, grabbing his arm and shaking it. "Did you say you bought Turtle Island?"

"I sure did. We can all go out there when we want and no one can say anything. It's ours."

"Wow! I leave for a few days and everything changes," Jenny declared, leaning back on Levi. "He told me about you putting up a tree and Sandy spending Christmas, but nothing else." She looked up at Levi. "You need to keep up with what's going on around here when I'm away."

"It's not easy with Quaid around. Besides, I hope you're not away anymore."

"Me too," she said, looking back at Quaid with a grin on her face.

Levi's stomach growled. "I hear you're hungry," Sandy laughed. "Come on, Jenny, let's get everything ready."

"Do you need any help," Quaid called out.

"No help needed," Jenny assured. "We can handle this."

"You pulled this off," Levi began. "I can't believe you own Turtle Island and you're getting married. Wasn't it only a week ago you were sitting here feeling sorry for yourself on your birthday, whining about life's what ifs, acting like an old man?"

"Yep, it sure was. I've learned a lesson. You can be mad at fate, an awful waste of your life or you can let go," Quaid confessed, leaning over cupping his trembling hands together.

"I agree, life shouldn't be all that complicated," Levi offered.

"Come on and sit down, dinner's ready," Sandy announced.

The men sat down at the small table full of food. Sandy poured Quaid, Jenny and herself some wine and Jenny got Levi a soda.

"I'd like to say a prayer, if you don't mind?" Jenny spoke to the group.

"Sure," Quaid answered, looking over at her.

"Lord, bless this food and please keep Kevin safe. Also, bless us friends from our youth, be with Sandy and Quaid as they start their new life and help them as they fight their battles in the coming year. Amen."

Quaid looked over at her with tears brimming in his eyes. She knew both of their secrets.

Levi leaned back in his kitchen chair. "The meal was delicious. I can't believe I ate so much."

"I can't believe you did either," Jenny said, giving him a look.

"I've been eating casseroles for the last week. I needed fresh home cooking," he laughed reaching over to her.

"You're spoiled," Jenny added.

"Yep and I love it," Levi said.

Jenny scooted her chair back and stood up, picking up the plates.

"Jenny, we'll clean the kitchen in a little while," Quaid assured.

"Let's put the food away at least," Jenny added. "I don't want to leave a mess.

"Cleaning up won't be hard." Sandy slid her chair back. "We need to put the lids back on the dishes and put the food in the refrigerator."

Quaid and Levi sat down in the chairs in front of the fireplace.

"The tree turned out great," Levi offered. "I knew you'd do a great job."

"It did and thanks for your help or it wouldn't have," Quaid admitted. "I would have had the tree leaning sideways, all messed up."

The girls came into the room and Quaid got down on his knees and pulled out two gifts from under the tree, handing one to Levi and one to Jenny.

"Quaid," Jenny protested. "I didn't have time to get presents.

"We've had plenty gifts this year," Quaid assured. "Don't worry about bringing us gifts. You know this is what Christmas is all about, surprises."

Levi quickly ripped open his gift. "Quaid, this is too much. I don't have any fishing tackle this nice."

"Well, you do now," Quaid laughed. "And so does Amos."

"You got Daddy some of these?"

"Yep, and you can take his and Georgina's present with you if you want. I also got Abigail a present. I do need to go see her soon."

Jenny was carefully tearing open her gift. "Don't worry about the paper," Quaid said, squeezing his lips together. "I wrapped the gift," he admitted, "not well, though."

"It's beautiful," Jenny assured him with a smile. "Oh, my," she said, gulping for air as tears ran down her face as she carefully held up the painting. "Quaid, this is too much. Your paintings go for a lot of money. I can't accept this."

"Oh, yes you can," he stood, moving over by her.

She threw her arms around him as tears flowed down her face.

"I don't know why it took me so long to give you one of my paintings."

"But you did years ago," she sniffed. "I have one of your first painting when you were ten years old. It's hanging in our bedroom."

"You kept one of those old paintings?"

"Of course. I have a few of the ones you helped me with, too, hanging in the hallway," she added, grinning.

"Jenny, you need to start drawing again. Sandy wants me to try to paint. I have a studio upstairs and you're welcome to come over."

"Quaid, you're really going to try and paint again? That's wonderful."

"My painting won't be like they were before."

"It won't matter, don't you see, it'll be like when you first started to paint. You painted then because you loved to paint, and you only painted what you wanted to paint."

"My paintings were so simple and I had so much fun learning to paint."

"Yes, you did and now you will be painting for fun again, not for the world to judge you."

"Jenny, you can struggle along with me. If I can try, so can you."

"I just might take you up on drawing again if you'll help me, " she pleaded, holding onto the painting. "I do love to draw."

"Of course, I'll help you," Quaid said, overwhelmed she'd ask.

"Now that's a painting. When did you do it?" Jenny questioned, moving over, looking up above the mantel, studying the painting.

"Back during our summer," Quaid said. "Levi, did you tell her?"

"No, Quaid," Levi answered, leaning back in his chair, watching the fire.

"No one had to tell me anything. I could tell you painted it the first time I saw it," Jenny assured, moving even closer.

Levi sat up in his chair as he watched his wife study the painting.

"Look," she squealed, her fingers waving in the air. "You put Sandy's name in the grass by the dunes. I can see it as it waves in the wind."

Levi started laughing. "I told you," he exclaimed.

"What?" Jenny turned around looking at him.

"Quaid told me the painting had hidden messages in it and I couldn't find any of them. Nobody else could either, but you did."

"I know how Quaid paints. Are there more hidden words?" she questioned, getting excited.

"Yep," Quaid leaned back in the chair with Sandy laying on him.

"I'll find the rest the next time we come over. We need to leave soon. We're going to go by and see Amos and Georgina this evening and then Kevin and I are going over to see Mama in the morning."

"Levi," Quaid added. "Get those gifts for everyone out from under the tree. Jenny," Quaid said, pulling her close, "Merry Christmas."

"Merry Christmas, Quaid," Jenny pulled herself up, kissing him on the cheek. "Thank you for the painting," she said softly, wrapping her arms around his neck and hugging her old friend, "It's nice to have you home."

"It's nice to be home," he assured.

Sandy and Quaid stood at the door watching their friends drive away.

"The wedding is going to be wonderful with Jenny helping," Sandy said softly.

"Yes, it is. Everything is going to be wonderful."

DIANN SHADDOX

A Faded Cottage

A Southern Snow

Sandy, you need to sit down and rest," Quaid urged, leading her over to her chair, laying her new shawl over her shoulders. "You've been doing too much today, not relaxing like you should."

"I need to clean the kitchen," she insisted, starting to get back up out of the chair.

"No, you rest. I'll see to the kitchen," he said caringly, kicking off his shoes, walking quietly in his socks. He looked down at his toes and grinned. At least he didn't have holes in his socks.

He could see how tired Sandy was from the busy day. He reached over and turned on the Christmas music, letting it softly flow in the room. Quietly he walked to the kitchen leaving her sitting in the chair in the living room; her head leaned to the side, watching the flickering fire. After a few minutes, he peeked back into the living room seeing Rembrandt and Sandy were both asleep.

The small kitchen table was overflowing with dishes. He tried to be quiet, but his hands didn't corporate, clanking the dishes and glasses as he rinsed them, placing them into the dishwasher. He wiped his hands on the dishtowel, closing the dishwasher's door. He switched the bright ceiling light off leaving the light over the stove softly lighting the room. He walked into the living room. The tree lights were shining on Sandy face as she took soft breaths. At least she was sleeping peacefully. Rembrandt looked up at him and he leaned down petting him as the tired dog's head dropped down on the braided rug.

Quaid's mind wondered about Sandy's Christmas gift; the paints, and canvases. He stood watching her sleep. He couldn't have been any calmer looking down at his hands doing a light flutter. He turned to the stairs and softly stepped into the dark world upstairs.

He flicked on the ceiling light in the bedroom and his eyes moved to the side of the room. Sitting there waiting for him were the easel and paints. He lifted a blank canvas up to the easel, carefully opening the paints and taking in all the colors. He picked up a brush holding it in his trembling hand. This was like breathing to him, not having to think. He understood how Sandy felt, wanting him along with her to fight fate and not let it win.

ET wouldn't kill him, but as years went by, he'd heard stories about ET becoming debilitating affecting his speech and his ability to walk. He'd hidden from his problem pulling his head back like a turtle, but not anymore. He wasn't going to hide from people. He was going to be a fighter as Sandy wanted and not worry what others thought. He was going to let the world know about his problem.

Quaid's quavering hand moved with ease. His strokes weren't perfect, scribbly, but the gift of painting was there. The colors began to blend with the precision of years of experience. He stood there in the quiet room listening to the waves outside on the beach as they chased the sand. With every stroke of the brush, the blue waves with their white tips began lapping at the shore and the sand sparkled in the sun's rays, bringing the painting to life. He could hear the words from Professor Kerrigan. "Never step back and second guess your work. Stay true to your art."

His body felt calm. The painting wasn't going to be a masterpiece. It was flawed, like him. But he would do as Professor Kerrigan said and he'd paint a small amount each day, not overworking his hands. He sat down on the bed. He stared at his work, taking in each brush stroke. For the first time in his life, he would try and not be so critical, judging his work. He cleaned his brush meticulously before putting the paints away. The easel was turned away from the door, he didn't want anyone to see his work. Not yet.

He stepped back into the living room seeing it was twelve thirty.

"Rembrandt," he whispered, the dog looked up. "Come on, it's time to go out."

The dog followed him to the door, running past, but was quickly back inside. The night air was getting colder. Quaid bent down switching off the Christmas tree lights, leaving the dim light of the lamp illuminating the room. The calming Christmas music became quiet. He hated to, but he leaned in to Sandy. "It's time for bed," he said in a quiet voice.

She wiggled and her green eyes looked up at him then back at the clock on the mantel. "Oh, it's late. I slept too long."

"No, I said you're getting rest."

She stood. Quaid wrapped his arms around her, leading her to the bedroom. She changed into her pj's and climbed into the bed.

Quaid pulled the covers over her bringing her close to him. Rembrandt leaped up on his quilt, scratching to get comfortable.

Sandy snuggled close to Quaid drifting off to sleep.

The next morning Rembrandt jumped off the bed standing next to Quaid, pushing his nose against Quaid's arm, waking him. Quaid peered over seeing Sandy sleeping peacefully. He gently slipped out of bed. He pulled his jeans and shirt off the back of the chair, slipping them on, going to the kitchen.

He opened the back door and Rembrandt stopped. The dog didn't move. Lying on the sea grass and in the trees was a light layer of

163

white snow. The flakes were gently floating down from the sky. Rembrandt jumped like a pup off the porch, snapping at the snowflakes hitting him in his face.

Quaid stood at the door amazed. The world was still, a silence had fallen over the beach, over the world. Rembrandt ran up on the porch, shaking the wet snow from his fur, quickly running inside.

Quaid hurried to the front porch piling wood in his arms. He laid the dry logs on the grate lighting the kindling under them bringing warmth into the room. He sat sipping his coffee.

"Good morning," came a voice from the bedroom. "Oh, it's chilly this morning." Sandy wrapped her arms around her body with the sleeves of her t-shirt gripped over her hands.

"You need to look out the window," Quaid said excitedly, setting his cup of coffee on the table.

The curtains slid to each side. "Oh, my goodness, it's snowing. They were right. It's beautiful. A day late for a white Christmas, but that's alright," she added, smiling, "A southern snow."

"Yes, a southern snow. It's cold over there by the window come and sit by the fire."

"Oh, it's so beautiful. I'm going to leave the curtains open for us to watch."

"I remember when it would snow in New York. The city would become calm for a while with everyone watching." He stood from his chair. "Let me get you a cup of coffee."

Sandy sipped the warm liquid, snuggling deep into the chair, her eyes glued to the window.

"I told Jenny I want a small ceremony on the beach. I think Levi, Jenny, the preacher, and us. Is that alright?"

"Whatever you want. What do you want me to wear? I do have a suit and a tux."

"No, I want you to wear jeans and a nice shirt. I want us to be free."

"Sounds good to me, but what did Jenny say?"

"She wants the works, dress, tux, everything. I think she's thinking more of what she wanted. They had a small ceremony and she didn't have a long dress."

Maybe we need to have a wedding for them on their anniversary. I think Jenny would like a new wedding, but I don't think Levi would," Quaid added, laughing.

"Not a bad idea," Sandy replied as she held onto the warm cup of coffee.

The mornings were great for Sandy. She had energy and today was even better since she was busy watching the snow. After breakfast, she came out of the bedroom layered in clothes looking like a robot. "Let's go outside. I want to take a walk on the beach."

Quaid grabbed his jacket and gloves, worried about Sandy being out in the cold, but he wasn't going to say no. He wrapped his arm around her and they stepped out into the winter wonderland.

"Wow," she shouted as she swirled around, staring up into the clouds, letting the snowflakes float down on her face. "I feel like I'm in a winter snow globe."

Quaid stood on the porch steps watching her play.

Sandy reached over, cupping her hands, lifting the pure white snow from the limb of the old oak. She spun around with a grin on her face, hurling a snowball in the air at Quaid.

"Oh, no. You can't win at this game," he yelled, scooping the snow from the railing of the porch.

She giggled, ducking as the snowball swished by. Rembrandt barked, leaping in the air.

"Alright, I give, you win," she said grinning, holding a hidden handful of snow cupped in her hand behind her back.

"Right," he laughed, seeing the snowball fly at him.

"I don't like losing," she said, wrinkling her flushed face.

"Come on, it's getting cold out here."

They stepped into the kitchen feeling the warmth of the fire.

"We need a shower to warm up and we need to put on some dry clothes," Quaid announced.

"To warm up, right," she giggled, following him into the bedroom.

The snow continued to fall for the rest of the day, gently floating down from the heavens. Sandy and Jenny sat talking on the phone like young schoolgirls, planning the wedding.

Quaid left Sandy sitting in front of the fireplace talking on the phone as he quietly stepped up the stairs. He stared in amazement out the French doors.

They say there aren't any snowflakes the same, another miracle like the grains of sand. His next painting, if there happened to be a next, would have to be one of snow on the beach, an unusual sight. A smile came over his face. Sandy was correct, a southern snow. He didn't pick up the paintbrush, not this morning. Night was to become his time alone in his studio, after Sandy was asleep.

"Jenny said we need to get the marriage license tomorrow," Sandy announced, hearing him stepping down the stairs. "She's calling her preacher, Brother John, to perform the ceremony, if that's alright?" Sandy questioned, her eyes sparkling with excitement.

"I'm fine with whatever you want."

"We also have to run by the jewelry store and pick up our wedding rings," she offered.

"Wedding rings sound nice," he added, rubbing his finger on his left hand.

Sandy and Quaid sat in front of the fire for the rest of the afternoon bringing up tales from their summer so long ago. Each day of their summer was like a year of their lives as they remembered details of each and every day.

Rembrandt ran to the door wanting to go outside. Quaid opened the back door and Sandy snuggled next to him. He wrapped his arm around her bringing her close, letting the cold air hit their faces. They didn't move, watching a phenomenon, snow falling silently, landing and melting on the warm sand.

Quaid pulled the door closed and turned around. Sandy's arms reached around him cuddling against his body. She looked up at him and he leaned down, kissing her, an avalanche of sensation overcoming them. She reached up and touched his face as he held her tighter. She wasn't worried about the what ifs. She was living in the moment. Her dream, now their dream.

His passion for her was like his paintings, so effortless, so natural. He pulled the covers back, slipping out of the bed as she slept quietly. He was on his mission, going up the stairs. He was motivated for the first time in years, letting his strokes flow freely onto the canvas. He didn't even have to think, his hands seemed to do all the thinking for him, bringing the painting to life.

The next afternoon he held the marriage license in his trembling hand along with wedding rings. Karrie had pulled some strings, a little sad as she looked at Quaid. But the news had spread around the small town, the news of their love story. Even Karrie couldn't fight fate.

Each day warmed a little as the week flew by. Quaid was living in amazement, waking up each day lying beside Sandy, quietly watching her sleep, taking walks on the beach, sitting in the rockers on the back porch. He smiled, not letting the ghosts of the past enjoy their time in the rockers. He spent each night after Sandy went to sleep up in his room alone, letting his passion flow onto the white canvas.

They woke to a beautiful day on Thursday, an exceptional warm day. Sandy had energy and wanted to go for a walk, pulling on her sweatshirt with a hood.

"It's going to be nice and warm Saturday. I think we'll pack our basket and have lunch on our island. She pulled her arms from him. Oh!" she yelled, spinning around. "I can't believe we own an island."

"Yes, we do and Saturday will be a perfect day to go out to Turtle Island. I wonder how it will feel. We won't be sneaking out there. And," he whispered, "we'll be married.

"It's going to feel wonderful."

He smiled down on her, watching her excitement grow but his stomach was knotted seeing her grow weaker each day.

"I'm going to take a note pad and my camera and list all the plants and trees so I can study them. After my surgery, spring will be here, and we can spend all the time we want on our island."

"It's a date, Saturday it is," he said. His eyes stayed fixed, scanning out to the sea, watching the waves from their beginning, creeping, getting closer with their climax splashing onto the warm sand. Then, the waves would be pulled back to the deep sea, a mystery of the sea just as life and fate. His eyes narrowed and he drew in a deep breath of air, wondering with worry taking over, hoping their dream, their life together, would come true.

Sandy could see the anxiousness growing in his face. She looped her arm through his, knowing it wasn't the wedding bothering him.

"Jenny wants me to stay with her tonight. She doesn't want any bad luck. I'm going to miss you," she declared, squeezing him tight.

"One night away and then when you're done with your surgery, we're never going to spend a night away from each other, promise."

"Promise," she whispered. Her hands touched his face, pulling it down to hers, kissing him.

He followed her into the bedroom. He stood watching as she placed a few things into a suitcase. Loneliness was overcoming him as he lifted up her suitcase, carrying it to the car.

Sandy leaned down petting Rembrandt with those confused brown eyes staring back at her. She pulled Quaid close. "I'll see you in the morning. I love you." Her hand held onto the car door. "You're sure we're not dreaming? This is for real? We're getting married tomorrow, right?"

"Yes, this is for real, but I think this is still a dream." He lifted up her left hand. "You know, Miss Sandy Jamison, tomorrow you will have a wedding ring on your finger."

"Don't forget you will, too," she added, grinning and giving him another kiss. "I better be going, bye Rembrandt."

Quaid stood watching her leave. "You know, Rembrandt, I hope our dreams do come true," he declared, turning and going into the house wiping tears from his eyes.

The night was lonely and his body squeezed him making it hard to breathe. He hadn't felt like this since that summer when he moved back to New York.

Quaid did what he did back so many years ago. He picked up his paintbrush and his body became calm. He thought about living most of his life alone, traveling around the world, but now one night seemed like punishment. He didn't know how he would feel if he didn't have Sandy and Rembrandt to talk to.

Diann Shaddox

A Faded Cottage
The Sands of Time

The morning was like walking in mud, but all of a sudden, time seemed to spin out of control. He was as nervous as he was as a teenager, standing looking in the mirror. "Get a grip, Quaid," he called out to the man staring back at him. His hands trembled out of control right before his eyes.

"Quaid, you still here?" Levi called out, coming into the cottage. He laughed. "I thought you might have run for the hills."

"Yes, I'm still here," Quaid shouted, stepping out of the bedroom. "I'm so nervous and my hands won't stop shaking. Levi, this is a long time coming."

"You'll be fine. You know the girls have been up since dawn. I should have stayed over here last night. It was like being at a slumber party. They sat up talking most of the night. I don't know how girls can talk so much," Levi said, shaking his head. "I see Rembrandt's ready."

"We both cleaned up," Quaid assured. "Alright, what do we do?"

"We wait for Brother John then you'll be able to relax. Maybe," Levi said, laughing.

"Do you have the ring?"

"Yes," Levi assured, "calm down."

The doorbell rang. "I'll get the door. You finish getting ready," Levi assured him, pulling the door open. "Brother John, please come in."

The short man with thinning hair walked into the living room. Brother John stood looking over at the man standing in front of him. "How are you doing, Quaid?"

"I think alright, but my hands aren't cooperating," he offered, rubbing them together. Sandy and Quaid had a long talk with Brother John and had confided their secrets.

"You'll be fine, son. No one is worried about your tremors," the man said sympathetically, placing his hands on top of Quaid's hands. "We better get outside. I know Jenny will be ready. She sure isn't going to let anything interfere with this wedding," he said, moving to the back door.

"She sure isn't. She's been waiting for this dream to come true for years," Levi announced.

The warm sun hit the men's faces as they walked across the dune onto the beach. Quaid kept his hands gripped tight, trying to control them.

"It's a beautiful day," Brother John proclaimed, looking out at the blue sky and ocean.

"It is," Levi agreed, "a perfect day for a wedding. Sandy's getting her wish."

Quaid stared out at the water and calmness came over him minute by minute. The tranquil waves were softly teasing the velvet, creamy sand. Rembrandt wiggled and Quaid turned around.

There, walking over the boardwalk, was Jenny. She stepped by Quaid with a huge smile on her face. At that moment, Sandy appeared on the boardwalk with a fresh bouquet of colorful, fresh flowers in her hands. It was as if the ocean began to sing. The waves swished in a perfect rhythm with small splashes adding to the melody with each slow step Sandy took. Her soft, light green dress, matching her green eyes, flowed in the gentle sea breeze as she stepped in the white sand, her eyes fixed on Quaid. Sandy moved near Quaid seeing the distress on his face. She put his trembling hands in hers, gently rubbing them as his anxiousness disappeared.

Brother John's words flowed out over the water.

Quaid smiled, the one lone seagull quietly flew over their heads, and Rembrandt didn't move, standing next to them.

It was time. Quaid looked into Sandy's green eyes. "Our love began on this beach and with these rings, we close the circle we began so long ago, keeping our love everlasting just like the sands of time."

Quaid slipped the wedding ring on Sandy's finger and she held his hand steady, slipping his wedding ring onto his finger. He wiggled his finger smiling, feeling the metal around his finger.

Brother John pronounced them husband and wife and Quaid leaned in kissing Sandy. Their dream had come true. The small wedding party made their way back to the cottage. Sitting on the kitchen table with bright colored flowers covering the soft, white icing was Sandy and Quaid's wedding cake. Sandy held onto his hand as they sliced the cake and did a toast to a long and healthy life.

Tears ran down Jenny's face as she hugged her friends, hoping for a happy ever after. Levi wrapped his arms around his small wife, leading her out of the cottage.

Sandy and Quaid stood looking into each other eyes.

"Let's sit outside, Mrs. Witherspoon," he announced grinning, opening the back door, leaving the wooden door open for some fresh air to flow into the cottage. "It's a beautiful day."

"Sounds fine to me, Mr. Witherspoon," she replied.

The rockers moved back and forth slowly.

"I called my dad last night to let him know we were getting married," Quaid announced. "He said to give you a kiss and he wished us many years of happiness. He was going to tell Mom when she was thinking clearly." Quaid leaned over in the rocker. "My dad was happy for us."

"I understand he and my mom thought they were doing the right thing for us. Remember, regrets don't help anyone."

"We will have to take a trip to New York to see them. Maybe Mom will remember you. She does seem to remember the past."

"It would be nice to see her again," Sandy replied, leaning back closing her eyes.

Later that evening Sandy lay in the bed so peaceful, sleeping with the moonlight shining in on her. Lifting the covers, Quaid slipped out of bed trying not to wake her as he quietly made his way up the stairs to his studio. Rembrandt lay at the bottom of the steps looking up at him.

The ceiling light switched on and the darkness of the night gave way. He stood with his eyes taking in each brush stroke on the canvas in front of him. Most of the brush strokes had wiggles in them, but they were interesting, giving character to the painting, blending the colors into one. It wasn't his best work. Or was it? He kept studying the painting, another painting made from love exactly like the one hanging over the fireplace. His heart beat fast, a few more strokes of the brush and he would be done, adding his signature to the bottom. He held onto the brush with his hand trembling, hanging down by his side. The critics would have a field day ripping the painting apart, but that was fine. This was his painting only for Sandy. He could see the flaws in the art, but he knew he would continue painting, defects and all.

He pulled in a deep sigh sitting on the bed, critiquing the painting leaning on the easel. His hands were calmer tonight, lifting up the artwork, caressing the painting gently like a baby, another child of his.

He switched off the light, slowly stepping down the stairs trying not to wake Sandy. He leaned the painting next to the cold fireplace in the living room with the light of the lamp leaving a soft glow, revealing the soul he'd put into the painting. He sat back in his overstuffed chair seeing the spirit the painting contained.

"Quaid," he whispered into the quiet night, "it's been two weeks since you sat here all alone. I guess you never know what life has in store for you."

Tears brimmed in his eyes in the peaceful silence of the night. He smiled to himself, placing his elbows on the arms of the chair, wiggling his left hand with his right, touching the metal wrapped around his finger. "Quaid Witherspoon, you're a lucky man."

"Yes, you are," came a soft voice from behind him. Sandy sat down in his lap putting her arms around his neck, snuggling close.

He could smell her sweet perfume. He felt her smooth cool face with his fingers touching her scrumptious lips, lifting her face up to his. Warm sensations stirred inside of him. So much for being an old man.

She jerked away from him.

"Quaid! A new painting, you finished a new one!" She said excitely, climbing off his lap, squatting down on the floor.

"I was going to give it to you in the morning. It's called *The Sands of Time*."

"You finally caught the sand," she said, gently touching the edge of the painting. "The sand is flying like you love with each grain telling a tale." She smiled, looking back at him. "The fishing shack is going to be with us forever, no matter what the future holds. You even put our names inside. You can see them through the door. How did you do such tedious work?"

"I don't know how it works, but my mind overcame my hands. I guess you were right, I had to put my mind into it and," he paused, "our love."

"I can see the love the painting has. It's wonderful and I'm glad you added Rembrandt lying to the side of the fishing shack. The painting tells our story. I'm still in awe how you made the sand lift into the air so softly."

"There's a lot of imperfection in the painting and it's not as defined as I used to paint."

"No, it's wonderful. More wonderful than anything I've ever seen and you're not giving up painting, no matter what happens to me. No regrets, Quaid. Promise me."

"No, I'm not giving up. I'll always try and paint, I promise. And I won't have any more regrets," he said, not wanting to think of the alternative. A life without her.

"Quaid, you need to face the facts. My surgery might not work," Sandy's voice trailed off. "I don't want you to live sad. Please take care of this cottage and our island for me."

"Your surgery is going to work. You have too much to give and someone has to see to all the plants on Turtle Island."

She stood up from the hearth, looking down at him. "Quaid, you have," she began, but he stopped her, reaching over, pulling her to him, putting his fingers on her lips.

He whispered, "I love you and that's all we need. Our love, no more talk." He held onto her hearing the waves playing with the sand out on the beach as he closed his eyes snuggling close.

The next day was wonderful. The sun was intense. The small boat bounced on the waves as they slowly made their way to their island. Sandy leaned back on the side of the boat, letting the warmth of the sun hit her face. Quaid smiled seeing the broom lying next to her by the picnic basket. Her face was turning red from the warmth of the sun and its healing touch.

Rembrandt was sitting in the middle of the boat, his spot, leaning his head over the side. The dog was so captivated, staring down deep into the blue water.

They pulled the boat up onto the sandy beach in its special spot, tying it off. Sandy picked up the broom on a mission, hurriedly walking down the beach to the old fishing shack. The weathered door swung open and she stepped inside, the broom began to fly with Quaid hurrying back outside. She stepped out the door and bent down sweeping the steps clean, her finale.

"There," she announced proudly, leaning on the broom, "the fishing shack looks better."

Quaid laughed as the one lizard ran past her up the side of the fireplace. "He's waiting to see if you're going to sweep him out the door."

"Oh no, Captain Claws, you can stay," she said, squatting down next to the lizard. "Remember, you can see to the fishing shack when I'm not around." The lizard didn't move, sitting on one of the large round rocks, of the fireplace, opening and closing his mouth.

"I don't think he's scared of you. He seems to understand you."

"I'd never hurt him. He eats the bugs, a good food chain of life."

She leaned the broom against the wall in the corner. "I think you can build a few shelves over to the side so we can keep some things on it. You also need to fix the three legged chair."

"I'll bring some tools and a new leg the next time we come out here, it won't take long to fix. You know, others are going to keep coming out here, things aren't going to change because we own the island," he offered. Quaid tilted his head to the side watching the lizard leaping on the top of another rock.

"I know and it's alright. What if we hadn't been able to sneak out here, it would have been horrible. Let all the people come visit. I hope each one will enjoy the island as much as we do. I think I'm going to put a sign telling them to enjoy the island, but to please not disturb the plants. Maybe you can paint me one."

His eyebrows lifted, watching her. "You need to eat and get some rest," he said, worriedly seeing her face pale as she held onto the doorframe to balance herself.

"I'm living every minute and every day, don't fret so, Quaid. Stop worrying. Where's the carefree guy, the one who stares?"

177

"Oh, I'm right here," he responded. He leaned down pulling her close, sweeping her hair from her face. "I'm not going anywhere."

"After I eat, I'm inspecting the island and making a list of plants and taking some pictures. It will take me days to complete. I want to preserve all the thick vegetation and hopefully leave it undisturbed for years to come."

He turned back to the door shaking his head, upset that she wasn't slowing down.

He helped her down the steps. "I think I'll bring some new boards next time and fix the steps."

"Oh, I would miss you helping me down them each time," she offered grinning, wrapping her arms around him.

"Holding onto you and helping you down the steps isn't ever going to change," he said, softly bringing her close.

Sandy shook the quilt laying it on the sand, letting Quaid place the picnic basket on top. She pulled out their lunch, feeding Rembrandt first as they sat quietly with the salty sea air tantalizing them.

"This day is wonderful," she exclaimed, leaning back on the quilt.

"Look up at the sky and all the fluffy white clouds. God is giving us a beautiful day," Quaid assured her, lying back with his hands under his head.

"Yes he is," she yawned, lying back on the quilt.

He scooted next to her putting his arms around her body, bringing her close. She once again laid her head on his chest and quickly fell asleep, getting the rest she needed. He didn't move feeling her breathe, listening to the calmness of the day.

She wiggled, wakening. The short naps seemed to energize her quickly as she pulled out her pen, tablet, and camera. "I'll be back," she exclaimed.

"Be careful walking around the island and take Rembrandt. Maybe I should go," Quaid said, starting to get up.

"No," she said, waving her arm in the air. "I don't bother you when you're painting. You need to let me do this. Come on Rembrandt," she called out, walking away, "we'll be fine."

Quaid stood from the blanket shaking the sand off his clothes. He began to walk along the edge of the water staring at Sandy. Except for the color of her skin, it was hard to tell she was so sick but he knew the truth. Quaid's mind was throbbing with pain. *No Quaid, you aren't going to let her see your pain. You're going to live in the moment.* Isn't it what we all have to do in life? Nobody knows what each day is going to bring. Like Amos said, "you need to live in the present. Worry sure doesn't help anyone."

Quaid followed along the water's edge breathing in the sea air, listening to the seagull's squawking, fighting over a fish one had caught. He stopped moving, feeling the warm sand under his feet, doing one more kick, watching the sand fly into the air.

His eyes squinted, seeing far out into the wide deep ocean bringing stories back his grandfather Witherspoon used to tell of pirates and mates out on their ships. The stories that made him as a young boy want to become a swashbuckling pirate ready to fight other pirates with his sword. One summer he and his grandfather built a toy sailing ship, painting the name *The Black Shadow* on the side of the ship. They enclosed a note deep inside with his name and where the ship was sailing from. They place the tiny ship on one of the waves taking it out into the deep water.

His grandfather said if the ship found a current, it could travel hundreds of miles. Quaid always wondered about the ships adventure, hoping someone had found the tiny ship. His life was like that tiny ship floating along going where fate took him. Now, what did fate have in store for him?

He could see Sandy entranced in her work. His heart ached, full of what-ifs. He wiped the tears and the sea spray off his face. He couldn't think of life without her. The ocean was softly heaving, breathing with calmness. He made his way back to their cove; the waves teased him, licking at his feet with their cold spray making him shiver.

He smiled looking at the worn, multicolored quilt. There were many newer ones in the closet at the cottage, but they could never replace this one. Their love was so like the worn quilt. As long as there was one thread of hope, their life together would last forever.

His toes wiggled on the tattered quilt as they dripped, drying in the warm sun.

His hands cupped some fresh, clean sand, holding it up in the air, knowing humans hadn't touched most of the sand on this island. He sat deep in thought and spread his fingers as they trembled. It was a flaw he could live with, letting the sand sift through his fingers and fly into the air out to sea.

He stood quietly watching Sandy survey her island with so many plans for the future, busy writing down all the names of the plants and trees. His eyes were seeing the young girl from years ago, the one with so much passion for her plants. Her face was beaming with delight weaving through the brush, coming back to the small cove with Rembrandt still at her side.

She laid her camera, paper, and pen down by the picnic basket. She sat down on the quilt next to him giggling like a young girl. In her hand is one of her precious wildflowers the color of the sun. She handed the flower to him with a smile across her face showing her dimples.

"Quaid, you're still staring at my butt."

"I can't help it, nice butt," he said with a grin on his face. He pulled her close lying back on their quilt, pushing back her long hair from her face with those green eyes staring back at him. His lips met her lips, closing his eyes holding her tight, knowing at least for a while they could forget what lie ahead for them. The what-ifs of life letting their dreams come true.

"One more day," Quaid whispered, "even one more hour is all I ask for."

A Faded Cottage

Now

Years have gone by and I sit, this December 18th, 2012, on the back porch of the faded cottage, reading page after page in the old journal I wrote so long ago. This is my account of two people getting a second chance at love, the love of a lifetime, an unconditional love. The pages in the journal are worn and the writing is chicken scratch at best, as ole Amos would say, but it's written by the hands of a famed artist.

A smile grows on my face feeling the warmth of the sun seeing those green eyes peering up at me. I have relived that one summer day when I was a young man and those precious two weeks of my life over and over.

My life, I believe has been one of miracles. I did get to live a charmed life. With all the great accomplishments in my life and all the great masterpieces I've painted, there's only one thing I'm proud of, a love that has lasted over sixty years.

I flip to the last page of the journal, the ending. I lift out the lost letters, rereading the words I wrote so long ago when I was a young man of eighteen, words from my heart to my best friend, my true love. I softly lay the brittle letters inside the journal, next to the one dried wildflower and close the cover, hugging the leather binder tight.

The rocker is weaving back and forth. I lean back pondering my life of one summer and two weeks. My trembling hands closed one door for me, taking away my love of painting great masterpieces for the world, but they also opened a new one and brought back the love of my life.

My story hasn't ended, not yet, at least not as long as I still have a breath in me to keep it alive. This is my routine, ending my day staring out to the great Atlantic Ocean, listening to the waves and the seagulls squawking, swooping down catching their meal. The constant movement of my hands has grown over the last thirty years, along with the trembling of my head and voice. I now say yes along with no when my head tremors. I wake each morning standing in my art studio, seeing the sun meticulously rise exploding with colors, letting my trembling hands move adding the colors onto the canvas. My paintings aren't great masterpieces the critics would say, but for me they're amazing. A gift I was given from God. A gift I will use until the day I leave this world. A promise I made.

So many love ones have gone before me; my parents and even my brother Bradley. I have kept my promise keeping my mother's memories alive, telling Bradley's children, and grandchildren tales of their grandmother and great grandmother, an amazing woman.

My dearest friend, a wonderful surprise in my life, Rembrandt, who helped to show me how to love again, died five years after he showed up on my porch that rainy, stormy day.

I do miss ole Amos telling tales of when he was a boy. He died years ago after living a good life, fishing each morning, as he'd done as a boy growing up in the low country. Levi, my buddy, a man who accomplished more in his life than most, not materially, but a father never judging his children, a son helping his father age with dignity and most significant, a husband making his wife feel loved, died last year. Jenny stops by as often as she can, busy with her grandkids, but still she takes time to sit and draw while I paint. We both sit and reminisce about our summer so long ago when we were young.

I stand from my chair, letting the rocker keep moving, shuffling my feet as I slowly walk across the worn porch. I close the wooden kitchen door going into the living room. My old, tired body settles into my squashy chair. My elbows rest on the arms of the worn faded chair. My wrinkled hands lace together. I gently rub my trembling left hand with my right fingers, feeling the metal circling, telling me our love will always be endless.

The flickering flames crackle in the fireplace, warming the room, but my body shivers. A coldness is coming over me, a coldness I've never felt before. A lone tear runs down my face and my eyes slowly close.

I feel a soft, gentle hand touching me.

A sweet voice whispers in the quiet room.

"Happy birthday, Quaid."

The End

DIANN SHADDOX

A Faded Cottage

Essential Tremor

Also known as familial tremor, benign essential tremor or hereditary tremor, essential tremor (ET) is a progressive neurological condition that causes a rhythmic trembling of the hands, head, voice, legs, or trunk. It is often confused with Parkinson's disease and dystonia.

An estimated 10 million Americans have ET. People with ET are often stereotyped as being nervous, withdrawn, anxious, and elderly. ET is not confined to the elderly. Children and middle-aged people can also have ET. In fact, newborns have been diagnosed with the condition.

There is evidence that ET is genetic. Each child of a parent who has ET has a 50% chance of inheriting a gene that causes the condition. However, sometimes people with no family history of tremor develop ET. Many people who have ET become disabled at worst and feel frustrated or embarrassed at best.

Quality of life is a big issue for people with ET. Daily activities such as feeding, drinking, grooming and writing become difficult if not impossible. Many people with ET are too embarrassed to go into public and so remain isolated in their homes. Stereotypes shape the way we think about people and situations.

With awareness, people with ET can come out of hiding; live normal lives as anyone with a disability.

For more information, please visit:

www.diannshaddoxfoundation.org

About the Author

Diann Shaddox is a Native American Indian and a member of the Wyandotte Nation of Oklahoma. She's an author, book-lover, and she has ET.

Diann was born on December 18th in a small southern town of Nashville, Arkansas, the youngest and only daughter of William and Mary Ann Shaddox. But fate stepped in and William, a crop-duster, died in a plane crash on November 20th at the age of 25, the month before she was born. Three years later, Mary Ann, her mother, died leaving Diann to live with her grandparents. At the age of 10, Diann's Granddad died of a stroke, leaving her Mamow alone to see to her.

When Diann was in her early twenties, life changed for her. Her hands had begun to shake when she would do tedious work. No one could figure out what was happening to her and her doctors believed she was nervous and just needed to calm down.

One day, standing in a post office window in Louisville, Kentucky, changed her world. Diann wasn't able to fill out a simple form containing her name and address. She had to find her answers. A neurologist finally made the discovery that Diann had Essential Tremors.

Not letting anything deter her, she continued life with the determination she'd learned from her grandmother. She learned how to hide her hands in public, how to grip her drinking glass with both hands, and how to use her body for cover as much as possible.

Things seemed to be working well for Diann but on her birthday in 2010, her hands were shaking uncontrollably. That night as Diann sat in her office, her anger grew watching her hands quiver. For the first time in her life, she felt sorry for herself. The question of why, a question without an answer, played in her mind. The words began to flow and Quaid Witherspoon, a famous artist, was born. *A Faded Cottage* became an incredible love story, one about strength of mind to fight fate and never accept what life throws at you.

Through this process of bringing *A Faded Cottage* to life, Diann has learned so very much and finding ˈ   ˙ the ET awareness groups on the web and Facebook and talking, listening to everyone's stories so similar to hers, has brought calmness to her life.

Even though the stares will forever be, she won't give up. Diann is determined to spread the word about ET and she is going to help make it happen. For each book sold, Diann will be donating a percentage of the proceeds of A Faded Cottage to

For more information, please visit:

www.diannshaddoxfoundation.org

Diann has lived in eight great states so far in her life. South Carolina is now her home where she resides with her husband, Randy, her biggest supporter.

www.diannshaddox.com

A Faded Cottage

DIANN SHADDOX

A Faded Cottage

DIANN SHADDOX

CPSIA information can be obtained at www.ICGtesting.com
Printed in the USA
BVOW03s2154270414

351893BV00002B/25/P